The Hero of Ticonderoga; or, Ethan Allen and His Green Mountain Boys

John de Morgan

"Almost silently, with his stick drew the wallet toward him."

THE HERO OF TICONDEROGA

OR

ETHAN ALLEN AND HIS GREEN MOUNTAIN BOYS

BY

JOHN DE MORGAN

AUTHOR OF

"Paul Revere,"
"The Young Ambassador,"
"The First Shot for Liberty."
"The Young Guardsman," etc.

1896

CONTENTS

CHAPTER I.
AT THE COURTHOUSE.

It was a cold, bleak and freezing day, was that second day of the year 1764, in the good town of Bennington.

The first day of the year had been celebrated in a devout fashion by nearly all the inhabitants of the district. Truly, some stayed away from the meeting-house, and especially was the absence of one family noticed.

"It seems to me kind of strange and creepy-like that those Allen boys will never come to meeting," good old Elder Baker had said, and the people shook their heads, and were quite ready to believe that the Allen boys were uncanny.

But after meeting, when the social celebration was at its height, the absence from the meeting-house was not thought of, and Ethan Allen and his brothers were welcomed as among the best farmers of the district.

When the farmers separated on that New Year's Day they had no thought of trouble, and each and all were planning what crops they should plant that year, and how much land they should reserve for pasture.

The snow was falling fast, and the Green Mountains looked grandly glorious as they, capped with the white snow, reflected into the valleys the feeble rays of the sun which were struggling through the clouds.

The hour of noon had arrived, and the good farmers were sitting down to good boiled dinners, which were as seasonable as the weather, when the ringing of the crier's bell caused every man and woman and child to leave the hot dinner and hurry to the door to hear the news.

1

All public and important events were announced in that manner, and it would not do to miss an announcement.

"Wonder what is in the wind now, eh, master?"

"Cannot say, but it's likely to be important, for Faithful Quincy has on his best coat."

Faithful Quincy was the official crier, or announcer of events, and was a most important character.

He never spoke one word, though everyone asked him what he had to announce, but he stood as silent as a statue, and as rigid until he thought the people had time to assemble.

Then he rang his bell once more, and followed the last sound of the brass with a most solemn appeal for attention:

"Oyez! Oyez! Oyez!"

Three times the phrase had to be repeated. Faithful would not have done his duty if he had only repeated it twice.

"This is to give notice, in the name of his majesty and of his excellency, the governor, that all true and faithful residents of the Green Mountain district must assemble at the courthouse at two hours after noon, on this second day of January. So let it be!"

That was all, but it was enough to set all the people wondering what was to be heard at the courthouse.

They returned to their homes, and finished their dinners, scarcely noticing that the dumplings were cold or that the boiled carrots had got soggy through long standing.

At two a large crowd had assembled at the courthouse, and all were in great excitement.

It was just three minutes after the hour, as shown by the sundial, which stood in front of the courthouse, that the sheriff appeared.

Not a murmur was heard. Even the children were silent.

The sheriff was trembling.

He held in his hand a piece of parchment, bearing a big red seal at the bottom, and he tried to read it, but his voice failed him.

After several attempts he succeeded, and the people learned that he had received a proclamation from Gov. Tryon, of the Colony of New York, in which he claimed all the territory west of the Connecticut River, and ordering him to send a list of all persons holding land under grants from the Colony of New Hampshire.

The country west of the Connecticut, now known as Vermont, was then only known as "New Hampshire grants."

When the sheriff had finished he asked what he should do.

"Why did you receive it?" asked one of the oldest residents.

"It was sent to me as sheriff."

"Even so, but you are the sheriff of the district which holds its lands from the Colony of New Hampshire."

The sheriff trembled, fearing he had done some wrong.

"It is in the name of his majesty, the king," he muttered; "and I was bound to receive it."

Through the crowd a young man pushed his way. He reached the side of the sheriff, and in a mild but firm voice asked to be allowed to look at the proclamation.

It was no ordinary man who made the demand. He would have attracted attention anywhere, and among those who knew him best he was esteemed, though the devout believed there was something uncanny about him and his family.

He was Ethan Allen, the head of the Allen boys, who had stayed away from the meeting the day before.

"Men," he said, after glancing at the proclamation, "we hold our lands from the governor of the Colony of New Hampshire. Is it not so?"

"You are right, Ethan."

"We pay our quota to the expenses of that colony. Is it not so?"

"It is."

"Then we have nothing to do with the Colony of New York."

"Nothing, and never want to have anything to do with that colony."

"You are right, Seth Warner; so I tell you what we will do with this piece of parchment."

The people looked at the speaker, and wondered what he was about to propose.

When they saw him take a knife from his pocket and slit the parchment through the middle, they dare not speak, they were so astonished.

In four pieces he cut the proclamation, and then handed it back to the sheriff, who dropped it as though it had been plague infected.

Ethan Allen picked up the four pieces.

"You did well not to receive it. I have a better use for it."

He took out his tinder box, and after a little effort, for the snow made the tinder damp, he got a light.

This he applied to the parchment, which sputtered and crinkled up in all sorts of strange shapes, until the great red seal, the token of authority, melted, and the wax ran on the ground.

"Now, let the sheriff acquaint the governor of New Hampshire with what I have done."

Ethan Allen stepped down, and walked through the crowd.

Not one person spoke to him, his act had so taken them by surprise.

It was a boldness that perhaps was criminal, they thought.

"What think you?" asked one.

"It was awful. I wonder the fire from Heaven did not consume him, for the king is the Lord's anointed, and it was in the king's name."

"I wonder if they will hang him?"

"Who, the king?"

"No, Ethan; most like they will."

"I guess he knew what he was doing."

"Ay, and he did right. We want men of pluck like him."

"Take care, Seth Warner; Ethan may get into trouble——"

"And I will stand by him."

"So will I," said Peleg Sunderland.

"And here is another," spoke up Remember Baker. "The lad hath the right spunk. I like him."

There was nothing done that day but talk over Ethan Allen's strange and daring conduct.

For days the people spoke of it in bated breath, for they had never heard of such opposition to authority in the district, and they were afraid of the consequences.

Gov. Wentworth, of New Hampshire, issued a counter proclamation, in which he said that King Charles had never given the land to New York.

The governor of New York appealed to King George, and he decided in favor of New York, and so, at the end of six years, the battle of titles stood just where it did when Ethan Allen tore up the proclamation.

CHAPTER II.
THE GREEN MOUNTAIN BOYS.

"What news?"

"Welcome back, Ethan. Is it good news?"

"Ay, man, tell us; what say the men in Albany?"

Ethan Allen jumped from his horse, and stood among his countrymen, the most honored man among them.

He had been sent to Albany to represent the farmers who held the lands from the governor of New Hampshire.

New York had commenced a suit against New Hampshire, and the trial was in Albany.

"Men, I know not whether you call the news good or bad, but it is just as I tell you; New York has won."

"And all our titles are upset?"

"Ay, that is just what it means."

"What are we to do?"

"I know not what you will do; I know what I shall do."

"What will you do, Ethan?"

"When the sheriff comes to dispossess me I shall be there with my musket, and if I fall Ira will be there, and if he falls Ebenezer will have a musket, and if he, too, falls, then John will try what he can do. That is what I shall do."

"But the decision says that New York is in the right."

"Courts have made mistakes before, and the strong right arm of good mountaineers have set them right."

"What said they in Albany?"

Allen told them of the trial, and then, with a glow on his face, he added:

"They told me that the gods were against me, and I retorted that the gods of the valleys are not the gods of the hills."

"Bravo, Ethan! you are a brave chap."

"If I had a score of men I would tell the New Yorkers to stay at home, and, if they did not, I would send them home."

"A score, did you say?"

"Ay, a score would do."

"Count me one."

"Just as I expected, Seth Warner; you know no danger when homes are to be protected."

"I shall join you."

"Why, Peleg Sunderland! you know what you will risk?"

"My neck, I guess; but, as I have only one, the risk is not much."

This was said with such seriousness that the people could not help laughing.

"Don't forget me," said Remember Baker.

"I shall be sure to remember you, Remember."

"If my man won't join you, I will."

The people turned to look at the speaker, and as they encountered the firm face of Mistress Cochrane, they knew she meant it.

"But I will join, Ethan," her husband, Robert Cochrane, said.

"Of course you will, Robert; but I don't know but I'd prefer a score of women like Mistress Cochrane to twoscore men."

Mistress Cochrane was a big, well-formed woman, and as her sleeves were rolled up above her elbows, she showed a wealth of muscle which many a man might envy.

Twenty men gave in their names, and Ethan was delighted.

"I'm proud of my Green Mountain Boys," he said, "and I shall be prouder still when we have won the victory."

"Hurrah for our leader!" shouted Seth Warner.

The next day Allen called his men together, and put them through their drill.

He wanted them to be soldiers, and so the discipline was strict.

He was elected colonel of the regiment, and Seth Warner was made captain.

The fame of the Green Mountain Boys grew, and many of the men around wished to join, but Allen had no idea of forming a large army, for his object was defense, not defiance.

He was sitting by the great open fireplace, looking at the blazing logs and watching the curling smoke ascend the chimney, when his brother, Ira, came in, and threw himself on the settee in the chimney corner opposite Ethan.

Ira was thirteen years younger than Ethan, but as bold and daring as his brother.

At the date of the formation of the Green Mountain Boys, Ira was eighteen, and as bright a lad as ever shouldered musket or hunted a bear.

"Ethan, I saw Eben Pike to-night."

"Well?"

"He wants to join us."

"Oh!"

"Won't you let him?"

"What to do? If we wanted a kitchenmaid he might apply."

"I told him I would speak to you."

"Well, you have done so."

"I wish you would admit him."

"Into the ranks?"

"Yes."

"My dear Ira, you forget that we may have to fight."

"I don't."

"What use would Eben be in a fight? He could run."

"That is just it; he might be serviceable when you wanted a message sent."

"I will see him."

Ira went to the door.

"Come in, Eben. The colonel will talk to you."

Ethan had no idea that the youth was outside, and he blushed like a girl as he thought the boy might have heard all he said.

Eben Pike was an orphan, and was not generally liked by the people of the district, simply because he was unlike the general run of boys.

He was very effeminate, and with his hair worn long, looked more like a girl than a boy of sixteen.

He was soft and gentle in his dealings with everyone. He had often shuddered as he saw a sheep killed by the butcher, and refused to hunt because it was cruel.

It was a strange freak for him to take, when he expressed his wish to join the mountain boys, and Ethan could not understand it.

"Well, Eben, I hear that you are ambitious."

"No, Master Allen, not ambitious, but I want only to be of some use."

"Can you fight?"

"I do not want to do so, but if we have to—well, I'd do my best."

"None of us could do more. Why do you wish to join the boys?"

Eben's face was scarlet; he hung his head, and looked very sheepish.

"Because, sir, the boys all say I am girlish, and I want to prove that I am no girl."

11

"But you might get hurt."

"I can stand that. When the bear attacked me last summer he tore pieces out of my thighs. Did I complain?"

"No, Eben, I will give you credit for pluck. As to joining us, why, I will think over that."

"Thank you. I am sure I could be of use to you."

CHAPTER III.
A CHILD OF NATURE.

Several weeks had passed since Eben Pike had signified his wish to join the ranks of the Green Mountain Boys, and not once had he been summoned to take part in their drills.

"It is always the same," he murmured; "they think me too girlish for men's work. I will show them yet that I can be of use."

Every day he wandered through the country, and even crossed into New York Colony, hoping to find out if any attempt was to be made to carry out the decision of the courts.

One bright day in May he reached Eagle Bridge, as the point is still called, when he saw a number of men carrying muskets half concealed, and walking toward the mountains.

He kept up with them, eager to know where they were going and what was their errand.

They sat down under some trees to eat their mid-day meal, and Eben crept close to them.

"We'll bag the two to-day, just see if we don't," said one of the men. "Zounds! I'd give a crown to have Ethan Allen in a line with my musket."

"You are more likely to look down the barrel of his," retorted another, laughing.

"We'll surprise him. You see, the governor has waited until the Green Mountain Boys, as they call themselves, got tired, and then he sends us; 'cause why? There isn't another sheriff in the colony as could bag a fellow like that same Allen."

"Do you know the way to his farm?"

"Yes, every turn in the road. We shall reach there soon after sunset, and then I'll walk right up to him, and say: 'In the name of the king, surrender!' and he will be so surprised that he will almost drop dead with fright."

"But suppose he is not alone?"

"He will be; at least, there will only be the young boys, and they will not fight."

"He will not expect us."

"No; and, seeing so many, all armed, he will surrender at once. Then we go to Seth Warner's place, and he might show fight, for there are two others live with him, but we will silence him by keeping Allen in the front rank, so that, if he shoots, he has to kill the leader first. Ha, ha, ha! It will be as good as play-acting, and the fun will be something to talk about as long as we live."

"Aren't you afraid to leave this wallet on the grass?" asked one of the men.

"I shouldn't forget it, for in that wallet is the order to eject and capture one Ethan Allen, a rebel and traitor."

Every word was heard by Eben Pike.

"If I could get that wallet!" he thought; but it was kept pretty close to the sheriff.

Eben crawled a little nearer, sheltered by the thick undergrowth of the wood.

He cut a long stick and-held it ready to use if he should be discovered, for he fancied they would not be very lenient with him if he should be caught.

14

The sheriff and his posse sat talking, and telling of their deeds of daring. Each one seemed to try to out-bid the other for bravery.

The conversation became animated, and a strange idea entered the listener's head.

He crawled still nearer, taking care that he did not move far without resting, so that he might be sure he was not observed.

He pushed his stick a little closer to the wallet, and found that he only needed to be six inches nearer.

After a little more inaction he wriggled his body a few inches farther, and then, quickly and almost silently, with his stick drew the wallet toward him.

He secured it, and fastened it under his vest, the safest place he could think of.

Backward he crawled, as noiselessly as possible, until he reached a clump of sumach bushes. Then he rose to his feet and ran.

Eben was a child of nature, and, as Ira Allen had said, he would be useful in carrying a message quickly.

He had been in the possession of the wallet less than five minutes when the sheriff proposed that the journey should be continued.

He sprang to his feet, and looked for the wallet; he could not see it in the long grass.

He felt in his pockets, but it was not there.

"I say, men, that isn't a fair joke."

"What isn't?"

"Who has the wallet?"

"Now, that's a good one! Who should have it but the sheriff?"

"Come, a joke's a joke, but don't carry it too far."

"What do you mean?"

"One of you has got the wallet, and the writs of dispossess are in it."

"I haven't."

"Neither have I."

"One of you must have got it."

"It's a lie!"

"Call me a liar?" asked the sheriff, of his deputies.

"If you say we have got the writs, yes."

The sheriff raised his musket club fashion, and would have brained the speaker had not Isaac Gerston, one of the posse, caught his arm.

"Father Abraham!" he ejaculated, "are you mad? What if the wallet is in the grass? Have you searched everywhere?"

The sheriff lowered his weapon, and all went on their hands and knees and felt among the grass, searching very diligently, but no wallet could be found.

A council of war was held. If the writs could not be found the sheriff would be punished. What excuse could be given?

"What shall we do?"

"Let us go to this man Allen's house, and surprise him. He will not resist, and we can take him prisoner, and in the meantime another writ can be obtained."

It was a risky thing to attempt, but there seemed no other course open, so the march was recommenced.

The loss of the wallet was a mystery. Not one of the posse believed it had been stolen, for they could not think a thief could have escaped detection.

The only surmise was that some squirrels had carried it up a tree. It was a ridiculous assumption, but the only one tenable.

When within a mile of Bennington Crossroads, where the Allens lived, one of the posse caught his foot in the root of a tree and fell flat on his face.

As he raised himself he felt something soft and slippery. He picked it up, and holding it above his head, cried out:

"The wallet! The wallet!"

The others, who had been a little behind, ran forward, and the sheriff at once accused him of having had the wallet all the time, and only when he fell and dropped it would admit its possession.

The man was indignant at the charge, but the suspicion was so strong that most of his companions believed the sheriff was right.

The latter opened the wallet and saw the great red seal. That was all he cared about it, and, placing it in his pocket securely, he very generously proposed that no more should be said about it.

CHAPTER IV.
"THE RISING OF THE MOON."

Eben Pike burst open the door of Ethan Allen's house without any ceremony.

Ethan and Seth Warner were sitting on the settee in the chimney, talking about the inaction of the governor of New York.

Off flew one of the bolts, and Ethan jumped to his feet and caught the lad by the shoulder, and was giving him a good shaking, when Eben cried out:

"Kill me if you like, colonel, but hear me first."

"Well, what is it?"

"The sheriff of Albany and a big lot of armed men are on their way here. I heard all their plans, and I have run all the way from Eagle's Bridge to tell you. You, colonel, are to be dispossessed first, and then Seth Warner, and if they can kill you, colonel, they will do so."

"Is this true?"

"Every word. I stole the wallet containing the writs, and here they are. I took them out of the wallet and threw that away, 'cause they might recognize it and find out how it was lost. Then I tore the governor's seal off the writs, 'cause that would be treason to steal them."

Eben handed the mutilated writs to Allen, and he saw that they were genuine enough.

"Will they come, now that they have lost the writs?" asked Warner.

"Yes, they will make believe they have got them."

"Then we must rally all the boys. Eben, you are a brave boy."

"Thank you, colonel. Do you want to shake me now?"

"No, my boy, and you can break off the bolts from every door in the house if you like."

"I'll go and fetch the boys."

"You are tired."

"No, Col. Allen, running never tired me yet. Let Ira go one way and I will go the other, for no time must be lost."

"You ought to be a general; you know just what should be done."

If Eben had been tired, those words of praise would have been enough to take away all feeling of fatigue.

Ethan made out a list of the men he wanted and gave each boy a copy.

"Keep as quiet as you can. Whisper your instructions. All you need say is, 'The moon will rise tonight,' and then the answer will be, 'At what time?' to which you will reply, 'As early as you are ready to see it.' That is all you need say."

"Will they come here then?"

"Yes, at once."

Warner hurried home to see that all was in readiness there to withstand an attack, and he left a speedy messenger to hurry to Allen's house in case the sheriff should go to Warner's first.

The first man met by Eben was Silvanus Brown.

"Silvanus, the moon will rise to-night."

Silvanus looked at the boy for a moment as though bewildered, but that feeling passed away, and he asked:

"At what time?"

"As early as you are ready to see it."

"Good! I am ready."

Silvanus stepped quite lively, and Eben, on looking back, saw him going toward the colonel's with his musket over his shoulder.

The next farm was occupied by John Smith.

"John Smith, are you there?" shouted Eben, as he opened the door and looked in.

"Ah, my boy! What brings you here now?"

"The moon will rise to-night."

"Is that so? That is great news. At what time?"

"As early as you are ready to see it."

"Good! I would leave the best boiled dinner or get up at any hour of the night to see the moon rise. What do you think? Will there be any bears about a night like this?"

"Most likely."

"Then I will take my old musket; it may be handy to have."

A like reception Eben met with at Peleg Sunderland's and James Breakenridge's houses.

Within an hour thirty of the Green Mountain boys had gathered in the home of their colonel, Ethan Allen.

"Boys, we are in for it this night. Remember that it is your own kith and kin that will be opposed to you. They are brothers, all these Yorkers, and we do not want to be the first to shed blood; but if they fire, that will be our signal. By the great mountains! we will give two bullets for their one, and may victory be with the right!"

After giving instructions as to the mode of procedure, Allen told them how he had heard the news.

"Never let any of the boys call Eben Pike a sissy any more. He has won his spurs as a true knight."

Had Ethan not cautioned the boys against loud talking, there would have been a rousing cheer given for the youthful hero.

"Whenever we have to distinguish our hero," said Allen, "we will call him Eben Pike, the hero of Eagle's Bridge."

There is no doubt that Eben's face flushed when he heard the words of praise, but he could not speak a word, for his tongue seemed too large for his mouth, and his heart would beat so rapidly that it made him believe he was going to choke.

It was Allen's plan to hide all the boys and appear as though he was unarmed and unprepared when the sheriff came.

Seth Warner had returned to his colonel's house and reported that he had made all arrangements for a speedy message if the sheriff from Albany went to his house first.

Eben had slipped out and had gone to reconnoiter.

It was unknown to Allen, or he would not have allowed the brave boy to run any more risks.

"Where is Pike?" he asked, as soon as he missed him.

"He went out a moment ago," answered Ira.

And in another moment he returned, the perspiration running down his cheeks.

"They are coming!" he almost shouted, so excited had he become.

"Where are they?"

"Less than half a mile."

"How many?"

"Twenty, at least."

"You did not see so many before."

"No; they have another sheriff with them."

"To your quarters, boys; and remember, not a sound until the signal. When I say, 'The moon has risen,' be ready; and when I say, 'It is at the full,' fight like turkey cocks."

In another minute only Ethan and Ira were visible, and no one would have imagined, from the appearance of the house, that others were in hiding, well armed to resist the foe.

Sheriff Merrit was the first to reach the house, and he signaled to his men to come forward.

He rapped on the door, and Ethan opened it.

"Does one Ethan Allen reside here?" asked the sheriff.

"I am he."

"Then in the name of the king I am here."

"Pleased to see you, sir. But I cannot think of any business the king may have with me."

"I am a sheriff."

"Indeed! and I should fancy a credit to the shrievalty."

Merrit bowed. The reception was far different to what he had expected.

He glanced into the room, and saw only the younger man sitting in the chimney corner.

"You are a loyal man?" queried the officer.

"I am loyal to king and country," answered Allen, boldly.

"I am glad to hear that, for my business would be unpleasant were it not that you are loyal."

"Sheriff, tell your business without delay."

"I have a writ of dispossession, and I am to enforce it. It means that you are required to give up and surrender this farm, and afterward to make such terms with His Excellency Gov. Tryon as he may suggest."

Allen had allowed the sheriff to finish his speech. In fact, it really appeared to the Yorker that Allen was afraid.

"Let me see the writ."

"You do not doubt my word?"

"No, only as I am a loyal subject I have a right to see that the order is in a legal form."

"Oh, it is legal enough, and properly sealed as well."

"In that case there ought to be no difficulty. Let me see the writ."

Sheriff Merrit opened his wallet, never once doubting that he had the writs and warrants safe in his possession.

He drew forth the seal and was ready to drop with excitement, for the seal was all he had; the writ had been torn away.

"I have been robbed," he cried. "Gerston, I have been robbed!"

"That is a pretty tough thing to say. Do you mean to say that you have not the writ you spoke about?"

"I had. I have been robbed. See, that is the seal which was at the bottom of it. You see that seal?"

"Yes, but I am not going to surrender the farm unless you can produce the writ."

"You refuse?"

"I do."

"Then, by thunder, I shall have to arrest you."

"Indeed, you are mistaken. The moon has risen."

"What has that to do with the matter? I tell you that you are my prisoner."

"And I say that the moon has risen and therefore I am not your prisoner."

CHAPTER V.
DEFIANCE.

"We will soon settle that. Men of New York, in the King's name I call on you to arrest Ethan Allen, rebel and traitor. Kill him if he will not submit."

The sheriff's posse rushed forward, and Ethan stood in the doorway, unarmed, and calmly said:

"The moon is at the full."

Instantly the Green Mountain Boys filled the room.

They came from all sorts of hiding places and all were armed.

The sheriff fell back, but only for a moment.

Advancing again, he asked:

"Do you intend to resist by force?"

"I do. I shall fight for my home against the governor of New York — ay, against the king himself. Stand back! You have no warrant for my arrest and no writ of dispossession."

"I had, but I have been robbed,"

"A likely story that. If it is as you say, then you are not a fit person to be a sheriff."

"I own I was careless, but that will not help you."

"I shall not surrender without a writ."

"But you will be a prisoner, anyway, for there is a warrant out for your arrest as a rebel and a traitor."

"Was that stolen, also?"

"Mine was but a duplicate; the original has been sent by the hand of Sheriff Alston."

"Where is he?"

A man stepped forward and announced himself as Alston, a sheriff duly appointed by Gov. Tryon, of the Colony of New York.

"It is enough."

"You surrender?"

"No, by heaven, no! The Yorkers have no power over me. I hold my farm from New Hampshire, and only to the governor of New Hampshire will I relinquish it."

"Then we shall use force."

"So shall we."

"It is treason."

"It is loyalty to my country. Boys, these men are crazy; they are so because the moon is at the full."

Instantly the Green Mountain Boys were ready to resist any attack.

The sheriff gave the order to fire.

Both sides obeyed the sheriff, and a blinding smoke rose from the old muskets.

No one was hurt, for neither side liked to be the first to shed blood.

Another volley was fired, and one of the defenders was wounded.

At the word they rushed out and threw themselves on the sheriff's posse, and, with muskets clubbed, they drove the Yorkers back, breaking many a head and inflicting more damage than they received.

The Yorkers rallied and loaded their muskets.

Sheriff Merrit, with a courage worthy of a better cause, addressed his men.

"Yorkers, we must have the body of Ethan Allen, dead or alive. We must quell this revolt against lawful authority. Will you follow me?"

"Ay, to the death!"

"The courts have decided that the land belongs to New York; the king, God bless him! has confirmed the decree, and opposition to it is treason. Ay, treason, which our king has called upon us to stamp out. Are you ready?"

"Ay, we will give our lives for the king."

Ethan Allen knew that the very name of the king was sufficient to strike awe into the minds of the people.

At that time the king was looked upon as the anointed of Heaven, and only the boldest would dare to say a word against him.

Allen was too democratic to look upon George as infallible, and to him he was only the head of the nation, and no better than any other man.

But the mass of the people had not shaken off their Old World ideas of royalty.

"Boys, it may be that his majesty has confirmed the decree," said Allen, "but he was misinformed, and when he hears from our own governor, the governor from whom we hold our lands, he will change his opinion and secure us in our titles. Until then shall we defend them ourselves?"

"Ay, to the death," answered Seth Warner.

"Then load your guns, and let us drive back these Yorkers into their own colony."

The Green Mountain Boys fell into line, Ethan Allen and Seth Warner in front, and in that order they marched against the sheriff's posse.

Volley after volley was fired, and several on each side fell wounded, some fatally.

Back fell the Yorkers, and still onward went the gallant boys under Allen's lead.

Allen thought the march too slow, and he gave the order to go at double quick.

The Yorkers had but little time to load their muskets, and they had not the quickness possessed by the mountaineers.

The unfortunate Sheriff Merrit many times tried to halt his men so that they might pour a volley into the ranks of the mountain boys, but they had become too demoralized to make any determined stand.

Merrit, with the courage which almost ennobled him, snatched a musket from the hands of one of his men and, standing in the middle of the road, took deliberate aim at Ethan Allen and fired.

The ball went wide of its mark, but the intrepid sheriff loaded quickly and again attempted to fire, but he spilled the powder from his pan, and the spark did not fire the musket.

Then he clubbed the weapon and rushed forward to meet the brave leader of the Mountain Boys, and was within a few feet of Allen when he tripped and fell.

His musket fell under him, and by some unaccountable chance was fired, blowing off the top of Merrit's head.

The Yorkers were thrown in a panic by the sight, and ran faster than they had ever thought possible until they were over the border and considered themselves safe from pursuit.

The victory was with the Mountain Boys, but Allen feared that it would prove dearly bought, for the laws were so strict at that time, and all his party might be held responsible for the death of the sheriff, who, being a king's officer, was sacred.

He gave the order to march back to their homes and see to the wounded.

Only one man died from the effects of his wounds, though others were in a bad way.

Save for the attendance upon the wounded, the farmers of Bennington might have thought the fight with and pursuit of the Yorkers only a dream, so readily did they settle down to their farm duties.

Several weeks passed and no sign of any move was made by the Yorkers.

Ethan Allen had sent a full account of the affair to the Governor of New Hampshire, by the hands of his brother Ira, but save for saying that the account should be read carefully, the governor had taken no further notice.

Seth Warner had a cousin in Albany, and he induced him to send regular reports of the doings in New York, in so far as they effected the New Hampshire grants.

And during all those weeks the news came that nothing was being done. Ethan believed in the old adage that a quiet always preceded a storm, and he held himself in readiness to meet it.

The Green Mountain Boys were drilled regularly, and the watchword was looked for whenever any met the chosen messengers of the colonel.

Eben had proved himself very useful, but for several days he had been away, and Ethan was getting uneasy about him.

July had come, with all its heat and unpleasantness, and still Eben was absent.

That something had happened to him all believed, for he had never been known to absent himself from his friends for so long a time before.

It was on the tenth of July that Eben craved entrance to the residence of Ethan Allen.

"Where have you been?" asked the colonel.

"Do not be cross with me. I have only been doing what I thought ought to be done. I have been in Concord."

"What have you been doing there?"

"Keeping my mouth shut and my ears open."

"And what have you heard?"

"Much that you ought to know, and I will tell you if you are not cross with me."

"I am never cross with you, Eben."

"Then you are to be sent for to Concord, and will be sent as a prisoner to Albany. Gov. Tryon says he will hang you as soon as you reach that city."

"How learned you this?"

"Nay, should I tell you I might never learn anything more."

"When am I to be sent for?"

"The messenger is on his way. If you do as we would like you would not go."

"Why?"

"Because the governor will purchase peace for himself by having you hanged."

"Hush! there is some one even now at the door."

"Welcome, most worthy Talbot!" exclaimed Allen, when Assistant District Attorney Talbot entered. "What brings you so far from Concord?"

"A message to you, Ethan Allen."

"To me?"

"Yes, from the governor."

"A message from Gov. Wentworth is always welcome."

"It may not be so in this case. I will explain. An application has been made for your extradition by the governor of New York."

"Indeed! And what have I done?"

"You are charged with killing a king's officer and robbing him of certain documents which bore the seal of the Colony of New York."

"Of both of which crimes I am innocent."

"And so the governor thinks, but he has commanded me to explain that it is necessary that you return with me to Concord, there to satisfy the court of your innocence."

Ethan looked at Eben, and the youth made a sign to convey that the information he had given was correct and that treachery was intended.

"And if I decline to go?"

"You will not decline."

"I may."

"You must not."

"I may do so; what then?"

"Then I shall order you into arrest."

"And take me by force to Concord, and from thence to Albany?"

"If the governor so orders."

"Then go straight back to the governor and tell him that, with all due respect to him and his authority, I will not go until I am ready, and that if you attempt to arrest me I shall resist by force. I am a free man, and by the grant signed by the governor I am free from arrest unless the local tribunal so orders, and you cannot get any justice in all the Green Mountains to order me into arrest. So go back and learn that Ethan Allen can take care of himself."

"But that is treason."

"Call it what you like. I shall defend myself when the time comes, and will never submit to tyranny, even from the governor of New Hampshire, nor the king himself."

"But I must do as I am bade."

"Try to do so, you mean. Let me tell you that Ethan Allen is in the right, and the governor is in the wrong, and I defy you and all the power at your back."

CHAPTER VI.
BEFORE THE GOVERNOR.

Mr. Talbot knew not what to do.

Had he lived in the days of the electric telegraph he would have used the wire to obtain instructions. But in those days only a horse was at his disposal, and that was a slow means of travel.

He knew that he must act as he thought best.

If he offended the governor he might be removed from his position and disgraced.

If he offended the mountaineers they might make terms with New York, and New Hampshire might lose all the debatable land.

There was a degree of sturdy independence shown by the mountaineers which, while commendable, was slightly awkward at times.

It is in the mountains that freemen are born, and, as Ethan Allen often told the people of the valleys, the men of the hills were a race of free men, who could never be enslaved.

Talbot thought over the difficulty and resolved to try diplomacy.

"You hold your farm under a grant from Gov. Wentworth?"

"I do?"

"You owe allegiance to him?"

"Certainly."

"You ought to obey his commands."

"Stay! I am a freeborn man. I willingly give service where service is needed, I willingly obey laws which are for the good of all, but I never yet agreed to obey any one man, whether he be governor or even king."

"And yet you have no right to the farm, save such as you received from the governor."

"You mistake the position. The original grant was for a tract of mountain land. That land is now mine because I have improved it, made it of value, and all I owe to the governor is the value of the unreclaimed lands.

"Will you not go to Concord and obey the governor's mandate?"

"Not until the governor himself asks me. When he invites me I will go; when he only commands I refuse to obey. Return and tell him so."

"I dare not."

"Then stay here and you will learn what freemen think, and see how they act."

"I dare not stay."

"What a sorry specimen of a man you are. You dare not, forsooth! is that the expression of a free man?"

"You taunt me."

"Taunt you? No, I only say that I dare do aught that does become a man."

Seth Warner entered the house and was welcomed by Ethan.

The colonel told the farmer of the order received.

"Will you go?"

"No."

"I should say not, indeed. Let the governor come here if he wants to talk with you."

Talbot could make no headway, so he left the house in disgust.

He went to Faithful Quincy, the town crier, and bade him summon the men to assemble at the courthouse at once.

Quincy looked at the attorney and waited until the order was given.

"In whose name am I to give the notice?"

"That of the governor."

"Then, please your honor, you must go to the sheriff and get his order."

"Is that necessary?"

"It is, if you want to have the people assemble."

Talbot wished himself back at Concord.

With Quincy he went to the house of the sheriff and obtained his permission to call the men together.

Every man, it seemed, was at the meeting.

Talbot told them that he was sent by the governor of New Hampshire with a message for Ethan Allen.

"Then why don't you give him the message?" asked Remember Baker.

"I have done so and he refuses to accede to the governor's request."

"Then you may be sure that the governor is in the wrong."

"What is the message?" asked Peleg Sunderland.

Talbot told them all he was instructed to do, and a loud laugh went up from every man as he heard.

"So Col. Allen refuses to go?"

"He does."

"Then that is an end of the matter."

"No, it is not," answered Talbot, quickly; "you are all bound to give such military service as the governor may require."

"That is true."

"Then I call upon you to arrest and convey to Concord the body of Ethan Allen."

Seth Warner moved up to the judge's bench.

"Are you jesting?" he asked.

"No."

"You mean to insist that we shall do such service as you have outlined?"

"It is my order, acting in the name of the governor."

"Then tell the governor that there is not a man in all the grants that will lay a finger on Col. Ethan Allen."

"Thank you, my friends," Allen said, speaking for the first time; "I refuse to obey the order to go under arrest, but I will go voluntarily and tell the chief executive officer of the colony that free men are not going to be ordered about like lackeys."

"And quite right, too. We will go with you."

"No, Seth Warner, I will go alone."

"Excuse me, colonel, but we have something to say about that. We shall take a few days off and go to Concord."

And as Allen had refused to obey the governor, so the Green Mountain Boys declined to stay at home, even when their leader so requested.

On the next morning fifteen of the brave mountaineers accompanied their colonel to the seat of government of the colony.

It was not a formidable military force, but it was sufficient to show the governor that he had to deal with sturdy men.

Gov. Wentworth received the mountain heroes at ones.

Talbot told his story of how he had been received by Ethan Allen, and he did not spare the young leader.

Then came Allen's turn.

"It hath been made known to me that the Colony of New York has asked that I be sent a prisoner to Albany, there to be tried for certain crimes. Is that so?"

"It is."

"It hath been told me that I am charged with killing a king's officer, one Sheriff Merrit. Is that so?"

"You are rightly informed."

"Then hear me. Merrit died in New Hampshire, and, even if I had killed him, I claim I must be tried in my own colony and not in York."

"You admit killing him?"

"I did not kill him. His death was an accident. There are plenty of witnesses to prove that. Then I am told I am charged with stealing documents bearing the seal of New York. Is that so?"

"It is."

"I can prove that when the sheriff did unlawfully enter my house at the Crossroads he had not the documents with him, but he had seals only. Now, your excellency, I am here to tell you that I hold my land from you, that I live in the Colony of New Hampshire, and that the sheriff of New York has no right to invade this colony, and if I had shot him as he entered my house I should have done right. What have you to say to that?"

Gov. Wentworth remained silent.

He knew that Allen was right.

"Do you relinquish all right to the grants?" asked Allen.

"No."

"Then tell the governor of York to mind his own business. I have not yet finished. I am a free man, a subject of his majesty, the King of England. And, as a free man, I ask you, his representative, whether you have made a promise that I shall be surrendered to Albany?"

"I decline to answer."

"You were to get me here by a trick, and then without trial send me to Albany, there to be hanged as a rebel and murderer. All I have done has been to protect the title you gave me, and my own labor, and I will protect that labor as long as my arm retains its strength."

"I am no traitor, Ethan Allen. I would have given you a fair trial."

"You promised to surrender me."

"I did not."

"Yes, you did; I heard you!"

Even Ethan was surprised and startled by the voice.

Young Eben Pike had stepped close up to the governor, and was shaking his fist in his face.

"Who are you?"

"I am Ebenezer Pike, and I heard you promise that Col. Ethan Allen should be given up to Albany, and your secretary added that he hoped to hear that the rebel was hanged quickly."

"It is false!"

"Eben speaks the truth!" hotly retorted Allen. "I would rather believe him than anyone I know. He is a child of nature and knows not how to be false. I am here to tell you, Gov. Wentworth, that we of the mountains are ready to give our lives in defense of the colony, but we will not sell our freedom!"

Wentworth knew not what to make of such men.

He admired their boldness.

He was afraid to lose their services, for he saw that troubles were brewing that would need the aid of men like Allen.

"I will see you again on the morrow. In the meantime you will all stay at my expense at the inn."

"No, sir. We ask no favors, neither do we accept any. We men of the mountains are independent."

"As you please. This young spy will remain with me."

"Eben Pike goes with us. He is of the mountains, also."

"But I must know more of his methods of spying."

"Ask him what you please; but he must be free. If he is imprisoned I will call upon the men of Concord to aid the men of the mountains to release him."

"You are bold, Sir Ethan."

"I am a free man, and I allow no one who serves me to be injured without calling the offender to account."

"But if he hath broken the laws?"

"Then let him be tried and punished."

"That is all we intend doing."

"What charge is there against him?"

"That we shall have to determine."

"Until then he will stay with us. I will be personally responsible for him."

Nothing more was said, and Allen and his Mountain Boys walked out of the governor's presence, taking Eben with them.

"Talbot, I would rather have that man as a friend than an enemy," said Wentworth when he was alone with the attorney-general.

"It will be better policy to please Ethan Allen and his mountaineers than Gov. Tryon of York."

"I am thinking you are right."

"If we do not placate Allen he will make terms with New York."

"But would Tryon agree to terms?"

"The Yorkers would make Allen deputy-governor, and Allen could take all the land west of the Connecticut over with him."

"What would you have me do?"

"Send for Allen; make him a deputy in the mountain district; give him more power than any other man in the district, and then tell Gov. Tryon to capture Allen if he can."

"Your advice may be good; I will think over it and will decide before I see these men on the morrow."

CHAPTER VII.
AN AMBUSCADE.

The energetic governor of New York had a spy present during the interview between the Green Mountain leader and the governor of New Hampshire.

Tryon had made up his mind to use his influence—and it was great—to have England amalgamate the two colonies and make him the ruler of the consolidated district.

In fact, he had already planned a scheme by which all of New England should be federated under his lead, thus creating a vice-gerency in the New World which should be all-powerful.

To carry out this plan he hoped to embroil the governor of New Hampshire with the mountaineers, and thus, by creating dissensions, show to England that a strong hand was needed.

When his trusted deputy heard from the spy the result of the interview between Allen and the governor, he called his aids together and asked their advice.

"Wentworth will give that fellow Allen all he asks," he said, "and our mission will be a failure."

"Cannot we capture this rebel and carry him over the border?"

"If we could we should be masters of the situation."

"Then we will do it."

"How?"

"Leave that to me. You must not know anything about it or it will compromise you."

"But, Edwards, unless I know the details how can I advise the governor or prove to him that it was justifiable?"

"That is the very thing you must not do until Allen and perhaps his men are in New York Colony. Then you can boldly say: 'Here is the rebel; hang him!'"

That evening, when the mountaineers were smoking their pipes in front of the inn, a man strolled leisurely along the street and looked at Allen and Warner, who were talking together.

He retraced his steps and stared at the men, hoping that they would resent the impertinence; but Allen did not notice him and Warner only smiled to himself.

"Can you tell me where I shall find a man they call Ethan Allen?" asked the man, after passing and repassing several times.

"I have the right to bear that name," answered Allen.

"Oh!"

"Why did you ask?"

"I wanted to see him."

"Well, you have seen him," Warner said, angrily.

"And who are you?"

"A better man than you."

"That I doubt."

"Very well; you are perfectly within your rights."

"I know that, but I would like to know your name."

"Seth Warner."

"I am Jack Edwards, at your service."

"Very well, Mr. Jack Edwards, you can serve me by going about your business."

"So I will, now that I have seen you. Good-day."

Warner did not answer the valedictory, and the man stooped down, and, picking up a handful of gravel, threw it at Warner.

"That's for your bad manners."

Warner, quick-tempered, was about to seize Edwards, when Allen pulled him back. "Sit down, Seth; the fellow is only trying to embroil us, so that our enemies may get the better of us."

"You may be right, Ethan, but I have got that fellow's face printed on my mind, and when I meet him, as I shall, I will pay him with compound interest."

Edwards saw that he could not provoke a breach of the peace, so he walked down the street, wondering of what sort of stuff this mountain hero was made, when he would restrain his friend from avenging an insult.

Early in the morning Gov. Wentworth sent for Ethan Allen and told him that he should refuse to meddle with the application for extradition, and that Allen could go back to the mountains and defend his right and title to the lands in any way he chose.

"Go tell your men that I have created an office for you. You shall be called the high custodian of the grants, and whatever you think necessary to repel the claims of the Yorkers you can do in my name."

Thus we have seen that the man sent for as a prisoner, with a gallows staring him in the face, left Concord a victor.

The conflict between the two colonies was to assume a new phase, and in that conflict Ethan Allen was to bear a most prominent part.

The Mountain Boys did not believe in wasting time, so they rallied their forces and started back as soon as they had attended to their horses and provided themselves with provisions for the journey.

Allen rode first with Seth Warner.

"Seth, what was that man's object in provoking a quarrel?"

"I am at a loss to understand."

"He was a Yorker."

"Think so?"

"Sure of it."

"Then it was mere curiosity to see you, and when he saw you he could not restrain his temper? He wanted to fight?"

"I don't think so."

"What is your idea then, colonel?"

"He wanted to embroil us in a quarrel so that the watch could be called out and we should be placed in the wrong."

"Perhaps you are right. Anyway, we are rid of him."

"Are we?"

"Yes, of course."

"Do not be too sure. The Yorkers will be mad enough to follow us, and, if a chance offers, we shall have to fight."

"What do you think of the dispute with the king?"

"For my part, I think the colonies should have the right to make their own laws."

"The king will give that right."

"No. George has all the pig-headedness of his ancestors. If the colonies get the right they will have to fight for it."

"You do not think there will be war between England and the colonies?"

"I do not know, but if there should be I shall ask that our mountain lands shall be independent."

"With you as first governor."

"I care not for that. I only want to see the people get all they deserve. Look, Seth! What do you see over there?"

"It looks to me like a number of horsemen."

"Yes, and they are trying to head us off."

"Think so?"

"Why, look! Baker, come here. What are those men doing over there?"

Remember Baker shaded his eyes with his hand and looked for several minutes before speaking.

"'Pears like as though they were trying to ambush by the side of the road and stop us."

"Just what I thought. Ask Sunderland to come here."

Peleg Sunderland was a good scout. He was a hunter from Wayback, and could find the trail of a deer or a bear quicker than any man in the Green Mountains.

"Colonel, we are in for it. Them fellows are waiting for us."

"Dismount!"

The order was obeyed, though many of the men wondered what could be the reason.

"We will have lunch — —"

"But, colonel, I — —"

"We will have lunch."

"Eben, get onto the trail, my boy. Find out who those men are about a mile ahead of us, and report quickly. Take care you are not seen."

The boy started off in a direction which was at right angles with the road by which the men were camped.

Ethan Allen bade the men appear to eat, whether they were hungry or not.

He told them that he feared a surprise.

The mountaineers rather liked the idea of a fight, though the odds were against them.

Every man had his musket ready for use and awaited the order to move.

Eben returned and reported that there were twenty-two men, well armed and apparently waiting for the Vermonters.

"They are led by that man who wanted to fight you, captain."

"Are you sure?"

"I took his measure when he was at the inn and I cannot be mistaken."

"Then they are Yorkers."

"That is just what they are. And, colonel, would it not be better to pass them on the road to the right, and then return and fight?"

"No, Eben. If we pass them we will not return. If we are attacked we shall give as good as we receive."

"Fight it will be."

"Yes, Seth, and we shall have tough work before we are through."

"We are ready to follow you."

"Boys, are you all ready?"

"Ay, Allen."

"I think they will let us reach them before they emerge, and they will fire at us from each side; so, Seth, you take half our men and I will look after the others. You give back good answers to the men on the right; we will take notice of those on the left."

"All right, sir."

"Mount!"

The men swung themselves in the saddles as unconcerned as though they had been partaking of lunch and suspected no enemy to be on the lookout for them.

They rode forward, and were within a few yards of the enemy, when the Yorkers leaped from their ambush and massed themselves on the road.

"In the name of the king, surrender, Ethan Allen!"

"In the name of common sense, who are you? A lot of clowns from a country fair?"

"We are the king's good subjects, and command you to surrender yourself a prisoner."

"Stand out of the way, you fool, or I will have to teach you a lesson."

Allen had spoken sharply, for he was sick of the formality which prefaced the fight which was to come.

Both sides were well matched. All were on good horses, and every man possessed a heavy musket.

"Do you refuse to surrender?"

"A Green Mountain Boy only surrenders to superiors."

"Then we shall have to make you, unless you acknowledge us as your superiors."

"Men of the mountains!" shouted Allen, "ride through these fellows—ride over them if they will not get out of the way."

Edwards ordered his men to resist and to fire upon the mountaineers.

"So you want to play the part of highwaymen, do you? Boys, return the fire."

One volley was fired by each party, and then the two opposing bodies became mixed up in inextricable confusion.

Muskets were clubbed and heads were cracked as the heavy butts descended on them.

Horses reared, and plunged, and knocked down those men who had become unhorsed.

The fight was furious for a few minutes.

Ethan and his brother, Ira, were in the thick of the struggle all the time, while Seth Warner seemed a very Trojan in valor.

Both sides fought well, and had the contest been a short one it would have been impossible to say which would have been the victor, but it was prolonged, and the mountaineers had the physical stamina which the men of the valleys lacked, and the longer the fight lasted the greater was the victory of the brave followers of Ethan Allen.

Edwards was taken prisoner, and on the understanding that he would reveal all he knew of the plot against the men of the grants, Allen allowed all the others to go free.

Two Yorkers were killed, while Allen's ranks had lost only one, and he only wounded, though severely.

In triumph the boys returned to the green hills of Vermont, and were received with many congratulations.

CHAPTER VIII.
THE CONVENTION.

Edwards was brought to trial on the charge of leading an armed invasion of New Hampshire.

He declared that he alone was responsible for the foray, and doubtless his statement was a true one, though Allen did not believe it.

The district court condemned Edwards to death by hanging, for his act was one of high treason, and the sentence was sure to be confirmed by the king, to whom it had to be sent.

When Gov. Tryon heard of the fight and the capture of Edwards, and his subsequent trial and sentence, he resolved on two things. He would bring all the pressure to bear on the king that he could to prevent the sentence being confirmed, and he would capture Allen and his friends, no matter what the consequences might be.

A proclamation was printed and sent through all the grants, in which the governor of New York offered a reward of one hundred and fifty pounds sterling for the capture of Ethan Allen, dead or alive, and a further sum of fifty pounds each for the bodies, dead or alive, of Seth Warner, Remember Baker, Sylvanus Brown, Robert Cochrane, Peleg Sunderland, James Breakenridge and John Smith.

When the proclamation had been well discussed the people got another sensation in a counter proclamation, signed by Ethan Allen on behalf of the mountaineers, offering two hundred pounds for the capture of the attorney-general of New York.

Both proclamations started out with a command to the parties named to surrender themselves within thirty days under pain of the forfeiture of all their property, of conviction of felony and sentence of death without benefit of clergy.

These proclamations placed the two sections on a war footing, and Ethan saw that it was necessary to organize on a larger scale than had been done.

He consulted his trusty friend, Seth Warner, and as a result a convention was called at Bennington.

"It is no use calling on New Hampshire to aid us. We must rely on ourselves," Allen told all with whom he came in contact.

A larger number gathered at the convention than he expected, and his heart was full of joy.

He was the more pleased that he had called the men together, when, on the very morning of the gathering, he received a notice from Concord that the king had forbidden the colony to take an active part against New York in the matter of the grants.

In other words it meant that the king would protect New York and oppose all claims of New Hampshire to the lands.

"Men of the mountains," Allen commenced, "we are met to form laws to protect ourselves and our property. We must rely on ourselves alone. I think that the time has come when we should declare ourselves independent of any colony, and apply to the king for a charter."

"Good!"

"That is talk of the right kind."

"Why cannot we have our own laws, our own governor and our own army?"

"You are rather previous, Sunderland."

"Not a bit of it. I say that the king has never done anything for us, and New Hampshire has betrayed us into the hands of the Yorkers."

"We will call ourselves the Green Mountain Colony."

"I think, if you will let me suggest, that if we are going to have a new name it should be a pretty one."

"Is not the Green Mountain Colony pretty?"

"Yes; but I have thought that Vermont—it means Green Mountains—would sound good."

"Nothing could be better," assented Allen, "so we will commence our deliberations with the declaration: 'We, the men of Vermont, in convention assembled'; that will place our name above controversy."

"I propose that Ethan Allen be our governor."

"Stay, that will never do. The king must appoint a governor, so we can only declare our desire to be independent of New Hampshire, and until the king accepts our independence we must nominally recognize Gov. Wentworth as our governor."

It is not our purpose to give the proceeding of that convention *in extenso,* but this much we have given, in order that the whole country may know that the sturdy mountain boys talked of independence and liberty with spirit even before the Revolution began.

Warner stood on a chair and waved his hand for attention.

"I have heard," he said, "that Gen. Gates is pressing the people of Boston so hard that the English are getting themselves disliked in that city, and I should not be surprised if a rebellion was talked of."

"The sooner the better, say I."

"Yes; why should England govern us?"

"We are too far away. The king— —"

"Leave his name out of the question. We can be loyal to him, even if we become independent as a new nation."

"We want no kings— —"

"Silence!" shouted Allen; "I will not listen to treason to the king."

Warner continued:

"If the people of Boston talk of rebellion, so will the people of New Hampshire, and we Green—I beg pardon, Vermonters—we, too, can govern ourselves. Then, when two or three colonies show some spirit, New York will have to tackle us all, instead of a few mountaineers."

"That is for the future, Capt. Warner; what we have to think of is, are we going to protect our farms?"

"Ay, to the death!"

The sentiment was the occasion for such cheering as Bennington had never heard before.

"We will hold our lands, even if every man has to carry a musket when he plows the ground or sows the seed or reaps the harvest."

"Good for you, Warner! Now, then, let us have a good militia."

Every man present enrolled his name on the list, and a very excellent start was made to form an army to defend the farms.

The district was divided into two parts, the northern part of the New Hampshire grants being under the command of Allen, the southern under the guidance of Warner.

Rules were laid down for the guidance of the mountaineers, and as good a system of government was inaugurated as existed in New Hampshire itself.

The strongest contingent of militia was sent with Allen to the north, for it was thought that the next attempt of New York would come from the Champlain section instead of Albany.

Everywhere Ethan Allan was received with open arms.

The farmers had reclaimed the lands from the mountain sides, and made them fruitful, and it was extremely hard that they should be turned from their farms without receiving compensation.

Resistance was popular, and the men who had taken the lead in organizing the farmers were looked upon as heroes.

Allen had taken Eben with him, and the young lad was the most useful member of his staff.

Eben had all the faithfulness of a hound, with the sagacity of a trained scout.

He was invaluable.

In some of the districts it was necessary to conceal their identity, for until the sentiment of the people was known treachery might be expected.

The reward offered for Allen was a large one for those days, and was a great temptation to the poor, struggling farmers.

So the leader had to be on the alert all the time, and Eben proved his usefulness by finding out all about the men before Allen made himself known.

The Green Mountain Boys camped on the shore of Lake Dunmore, and made the place their headquarters for the district.

Eben was returning to the camp one night when he was accosted by a lad about his own age.

"You're a stranger about here, eh?" said the lad.

"Yes; just looking about."

"Oh, from New York?"

"No, I come from New Hampshire."

"So did I. I used to live in Concord. Ever in Concord?"

"Many times," answered Eben.

"Then we ought to be friends. Looking for work?"

"Partly. My folks want a good grant somewhere, and I'm looking about for one."

"There aren't many good places now; most have been taken. They do say that a man called Ethan Allen is round stirring up the people so that he may get them their lands free."

"So I have heard."

"But some say that he wants the lands for himself."

"How is that?" asked Eben, innocently.

"Why, I have heard a man say—he came from Fort Ticonderoga— that if Allen can get his way there will be a fight. Then he will surrender and will recognize York, and as a reward will get the best farms."

"It's a——"

Eben was about to give the boy a piece of his mind, but checked himself in time.

"It's a what?" asked the lad.

"Very unlikely story, I was about to say, but thought that I would not."

"Why?"

"Because a man who would think such a thing about Col. Allen is not worth contradicting."

"Oh, that is it. So you believe in this man, Allen?"

"I do."

"So does father. He says that he will stick by him as long as he has a hand to hold a gun."

"What is your father's name?"

"Why do you want to know?"

"Only he might help me to find a good piece of farm land which I could get by applying."

"So he might. Well, my father is Ezekiel Garvan—Old Zeke, they call him round about. Glad to see you when you are near. See, that is our house over yon, where the smoke is rising up from among the trees."

"And what is your name?" asked Eben.

"I am called Zeb; it is short for Zebedee. What is your name?"

Incautiously he answered, truthfully:

"Ebenezer Pike is my name."

The boys separated, and Eben returned to the camp, feeling pleased with himself to think he had found a good friend, as he never doubted old Zeke would be.

Zeb stood watching Eben for a time, and then he too returned home.

"My old dad used to blame me for listening, and used to say that little pitchers had big ears, when anyone was there, just to prevent them talking, but the big ears will be useful now, or I am not fit to be my father's son."

CHAPTER IX.
TREACHERY.

Zebedee was flushed and excited when he entered the paternal dwelling.

He had been away all day, and knew that he was likely to get a good thrashing for neglect of his work.

Ezekiel was waiting for him very patiently.

Zeb had taken all in at a glance. There was a thick beechen stick standing by the chimney corner, and old Zeke was not far from it.

One of his most favored passages of the Bible was the one in which the spoiling of the child is said to be caused by the small use of the rod.

Zeb knew what it meant.

He had often felt the strength of his father's muscles, and he fully realized that if he was spoiled it was not because the rod had been spared.

Only three mornings before Zeb had entered the kitchen, which served as dining room as well, and had partaken of his breakfast standing, and at the midday meal he still preferred an upright position instead of the one adopted by the other members of his family.

To be accurate and truthful, it was a rare thing for Zeb to be able to sit down with any comfort, for his interviews with his father were very frequent and generally of a very painful nature.

He entered the kitchen looking more defiant than his brothers or sister had ever seen him.

Zeke did not speak.

He took off his coat and rolled up his homespun linen shirt sleeves.

Then he reached out and got the beechen stick.

Zebedee waited.

He knew that there was a certain formula to be gone through.

His father never thrashed him while angry; he always catechised him, then waited a few minutes before plying the stick or the whip.

"Zeb, did you sort those potatoes?"

"No."

"Did you learn that verse from the Bible the elder told you to commit to memory?"

"No."

"Playing all day?"

"Yes."

"Then I must use the rod, or my son will be ruined."

Everything had been calm up to that point.

The other members of the family had gone out.

Zeb was alone with his father.

"Come here."

"What for?"

"Come here, I say, and place yourself across my knee."

"Not this time, dad."

If Zebedee had drawn a pistol and shot at his father that worthy could not have been more astonished. He almost dropped the stick.

"What do you mean?"

"Just what I say. You are never going to beat me again."

"What?"

"Just what I say, dad. I'm going to make a bargain with you. You swear that you will never hit me again and I'll make you a rich man."

Ezekiel dropped the stick.

He opened his ponderous jaws and looked at his eldest son much as he might at a wild beast.

"You—what?"

"Just what I say, dad. Little pitchers have big ears. Well, the big ears have heard that you hate Ethan Allen."

"Well?"

"You would get the reward if you could."

"Well?"

"Swear that you will never hit me again——"

"I will not. Come here, you rapscalion, and I'll teach you to make a laughingstock of me."

Zeb saw his father pick up the stick again, and he got into the corner, and picking up a chair, held it so that his father could not strike him.

"See here, father," he said, very quietly, "you are stronger than I am. You have a right to whip me, and I perhaps deserve it; that isn't saying much, but it's enough. Now I want to tell you that if you strike me I'll leave you this very night, and either join the Green Mountain Boys, or I'll get the reward and go to York and never see you again."

"What has come over you?"

"Nothing, only I see a way to make some money for you, or myself, and I'll give it to you if you swear never to strike me again."

"It's a bargain."

"Honor bright?"

"Yes, honor bright."

"All right, father. Pull down your sleeves and come with me where no one can hear what I have to say."

To the great surprise of the family, no sounds of crying or sobbing came from the kitchen, and when Zeb's mother—a little, frail woman, who had never had her own way since she had been married to Zeke, opened the door an hour later and peeped in, she screamed out:

"It's all over! I felt he would do it some day."

"Do what, mother?" asked a girl of twelve.

"Your father has killed Zeb. He said he would, and now he has done it, and he has gone to bury him."

Then there was a scene of shrieking and weeping and sobbing.

All the children joined in, and the mother was heart-broken.

In the midst of it all father and son walked in, radiant and smiling.

If Zeb had been really dead and made himself visible to his astonished family, they could not have been more alarmed.

"Mistress Garvan, stop your blubbering. We shall have visitors this night; sha'n't we, Zeb?"

"Yes, dad."

"Friends of mine. Oh, it will be a great time. Mistress, I'll buy the childer new clothes, ay, that I will, and I'll have a new ox for the farm. It is good, I tell you, to have friends."

Mistress Garvan wondered what had come over her stern husband.

She knew he had not been drinking, for he would not allow even as much as a drop of dry cider to come into the house.

"What have you been doing, Zeke?" she asked him.

"Nothing; it's only a little surprise we have. Isn't it so, Zeb?"

But Zeb had disappeared, and so no answer was forthcoming from him.

Zeb had seen more than he had heard, and he knew of the encampment on Lake Dunmore.

He had watched the men, and found out that they drilled at night. He had become suspicious, but had no means of verifying his suspicions until that conversation with Eben.

When Eben had incautiously mentioned his name, Zeb remembered that he had heard a man tell his father that Allen was accompanied by a young scout whose name was Pike.

Zeke was getting very fidgety.

He kept looking at the tall clock, which his father had brought from England many years before, and wondered whether his plot had failed. But his face brightened when a knock at the door betokened the presence of visitors.

He opened the door himself, and Ethan Allen and Remember Baker stepped in.

"Welcome, most welcome! I would rather see you here than the king of England."

Allen placed his finger on his lip as a hint not to speak too loudly.

Zeke laughed.

"I respect your caution; a day will come when your name will be shouted from the housetops."

"You are too flattering, farmer."

"Not so; but come to supper. My good wife knows how to tickle the palate of my friends, and you are my friends. Where's Zeb, mother?"

"He went out."

"He is a bad fellow; I am sure I shall never tame him. I would he were old enough to join the——"

"Yes; what age is he?"

"Only sixteen."

"He is old enough if he has inclination——"

"A truce to such talk; let us get some supper. By my father's memory, I smell pig's head and cabbage. Good thing, even if it is late at night. Come, friends, and we will talk after."

Zeke led the way into the kitchen and bade his guest be seated.

Scarcely had they commenced eating when a knock at the back door caused the farmer to drop his knife.

The door opened and a man's voice was heard:

"In the king's name surrender, Ethan Allen, and you, Remember Baker!"

"Treason!" exclaimed Allen.

"Trapped!" added Baker.

"Yes, rebels, and the reward will be mine!" shouted the farmer in a joyous voice.

CHAPTER X.
ZEB'S DOUBLE DEALING.

"Scoundrel!" shouted Baker.

Allen was dignified even under such trying circumstances. He calmly waited the pleasure of the soldiers, knowing that resistance was useless; but Remember Baker was impetuous, and would have fought even against such odds if he had not been overpowered.

"Have you any cords?" asked the young officer.

"Ay, faith I'll get the strongest cords that ye ever saw," exclaimed Zeb.

"You young imp, it was you who betrayed us," Baker said, bitterly.

"Yes, you are right. You see, I bear you no ill will," said the young scoundrel, "but money is useful, and they perhaps won't hang you, and if they do—well, you've got to die sometime, and you might as well make us comfortable by your death——"

Zeke was a little ashamed of his part in the transaction, though he had been ready enough to adopt his son's suggestion. But now that the deed was done, he would not allow the prisoners to be insulted by Zeb, and the boy's unfeeling remarks were cut short by a vigorous kick on his nether part which completely lifted him off the floor.

"You said you'd never—hit—me," he blubbered.

"I never said I'd never kick you, and I'll kick all I want to, you young rascal!"

"No, you won't," the young hopeful retorted.

"Yes, I will, and if you don't get those cords in a brace of shakes I'll make you so you won't sit down for a month."

Zeb knew enough of his father to be sure that he meant what he said, so he hurried to the barn, and soon returned with some strong rope, with which the two prisoners were securely bound.

The boy was a shrewd fellow, and as bad as any that lived in those parts. His father had not half the quick wit possessed by Zeb.

"Dad, get the reward," he whispered.

"Ay, who will pay me the reward?" he asked the officer.

"I will certify that you are entitled to it, and you can get it from Albany any time."

"Ay, so I must needs trudge to Albany. Must I go with the prisoners?"

"No, you have nothing to do with them now; they are in my care."

"So if they get away — —"

"But they cannot get away."

"But if they did?" Zeb persisted.

"That would be my loss. You and your father have earned the reward."

"Where shall you keep them to-night?" asked Zeke.

"I shall take them to — — Well, never mind where; it will make no difference to you."

"No, I suppose not."

Zeb overheard this conversation and determined to profit by it.

He felt sore, both physically and mentally.

He felt that his father had not kept to the meaning of his oath, and had evaded it by kicking instead of striking, which to Zeb was just as bad.

"I might just as well have let him hit me," he soliloquized; "he laughs now; perhaps he will not when I am through."

He ran, and none could go faster when he liked to exert himself, and did not rest until he was in sight of the Mountain Boys' camp.

Then he halted.

He needed to be cool.

"Zebedee, my boy, now you can make or mar your life. Which are you going to do?"

He thought for a moment and chuckled to himself as he defined, mentally, his plan of action.

Peleg Sunderland was in command in the absence of the colonel and Capt. Baker, and to him Zeb asked to be conducted.

But the sentinel refused.

"You haven't got the word, and I will not let anyone pass; no, not even the colonel himself without it."

"But I have important news."

"Of course you have."

"You do not believe me?"

"Yes, I do. I know all you can tell me, so there!"

"Have you anyone here called Eben Pike?"

"Perhaps we have, perhaps we haven't."

"Do not be sassy or——"

"You'll march away from this or I'll shoot; them's my orders."

Zeb saw that the man would not allow him to pass, and he was at his wits' end to know what to do.

As good fortune would have it, who should pass but Eben.

"Eben, I want you."

"Is that you, Zeb?"

"It is."

"What do you want?"

"You."

"What for?"

"Come here and I will tell you."

The sentry warned Eben not to pass out of the lines, but the young scout took no notice.

"Well, what is it?"

"Come a little farther away and I will tell you."

Eben knew not what fear was, though that was saying a great deal. One of the kings of Spain once sent for a man who was heard to say that he did not know the meaning of fear.

"My good man," said the king, "they tell me that you were never afraid."

"That is true, your majesty."

"And you do not know what fear is?"

"That also was true."

"Did you ever put your hand into a wasps' nest?"

"No, your majesty."

"Then never again say you do not know what fear is."

Eben might find something of which he would be afraid, but he had not done so up to that time.

When the two boys had got some distance away, Eben asked:

"Well, what have you to tell me?"

"Where is Col. Ethan Allen?"

"I do not know."

"Where is Capt. Baker?"

"I do not know."

"I do."

"Well, what of that?"

"When I last saw them they had some good strong cords bound round their limbs, and a Yorker was holding a gun at their heads."

"Prisoners?"

"It looked very like it."

"Where are they? Tell me all you know."

"Not much; the news is worth something."

"How much do you want?"

"How much what?"

"Did you not say you wanted to sell the news?"

"No; but, now you mention it, I might do so. Take me to the fellow who commands the boys."

"Will you tell him?"

"I came to do so, only that fellow with the gun would not let me pass."

"I will take you to Lieut. Sunderland."

"Lead on; I am ready."

Eben conducted the boy to Sunderland, and to him Zeb told a most wonderful yarn.

It was so plausible that he was complimented on his patriotism, and rewarded by the faithful lieutenant as well as his purse would permit.

Zeb trusted to the inspiration of the moment for most of his narrative. He told how his father was a loyal Vermonter, and in the fullness of his heart had invited Allen and Baker to a late supper, and in their honor had prepared boiled pig's head and cabbage, and that while they were eating supper some soldiers burst open the door and took all prisoners. Zeb said his father was released on condition that he would find ropes to bind Allen and Baker. Thinking that he could be of service to the colonel by remaining at liberty, he consented, and then sent Zeb to the Mountain Boys' camp.

Zeb embellished the story in many ways, but he was so good a story-teller that every word he uttered was believed.

CHAPTER XI.
THE TABLES TURNED.

Ethan Allen could see no possible chance of escape.

He was not afraid to meet the punishment, but he felt it galling to be trapped in such a way.

If he had not been a bitter opponent of New York before, that treachery would have made him one.

For greater security the two mountaineers had been bound together, so that they could be more easily guarded.

Nearly an hour passed before the officer determined to march.

He had sent out scouts to ascertain if the Mountain Boys were in the vicinity, and the men had returned to report all quiet.

Then the small company, with its valuable captives, set out to cross into York at the nearest point.

For about an hour the march was continued in silence, and the men were fatigued, for they had to carry the prisoners, both Allen and Baker refusing to walk one step.

A halt was called, and the soldiers were told they could rest for one hour.

They were delighted at the prospect, and laid themselves down on the grass.

So secure did they feel that they relaxed their watchfulness and allowed the prisoners to lie down by themselves a little distance away, yet not so far that they had any chance of escape.

Allen was singing a song of freedom; it was an old French ditty he had learned and often sung.

He sang, not because his spirits were light, but simply to prevent a feeling of melancholy overmastering him.

The singing satisfied his captors that he was resigned, and was not meditating any plan of escape.

In the midst of his song he heard a soft, low voice say:

"Do not speak, but listen."

Baker had fallen asleep, and Allen knew that it was Eben who spoke; but how the boy got there, or, in fact, where he was, Allen could not conjecture.

"Here is a knife," said Eben; "I am going to cut the cords which bind your hands; you can then liberate Baker. When you are both free, keep still until you hear the cry of the catbird, and then leap to your feet and run, taking a course direct to the left; the boys are there in ambush, and you will be safe."

While Eben was speaking he succeeded in cutting the cords, and Allen's hands were free.

Eben glided away as noiselessly as he came, and Allen woke Baker as quickly as possible.

"Heigho! Have we to continue our journey?"

"Hush! do not utter a word! We have a chance to escape, if you will listen and not speak."

Allen told him all that had been done, and then quietly cut the other's cords.

Both men were free.

They lay as still as though the cords still bound their bodies.

Allen sang another song in a low, tremulous voice.

Again it had the effect of disarming suspicion.

A bird warbled in a tree, rather strangely for so late at night, but as one of the men remarked that it was the bird's lookout and not his, no notice was taken of it.

And then the warbling ceased and the peculiar call of the catbird was heard.

Instantly the two prisoners were on their feet and making for the wood.

They had got some yards before their movement was noticed.

At once the soldiers seized their guns, and a volley was fired after the fugitives.

The shots did not reach the mark, and pursuit was commenced.

Allen heard the catbird again and again, and by its sound guided his footsteps.

The soldiers were close behind and were gaining every minute, but the Mountain Boys ran pluckily, for it was a race for life in reality.

They rushed into the dense wood and followed the narrow path, which was really a deer run.

Some of the soldiers fired again, and a ball struck a tree and ricochetted, injuring the leader of the little band of pursuers.

The accident made the men more furious, and they ran so fast that it seemed Allen and Baker must certainly fall into their hands.

Suddenly the scene changed.

From behind every tree there leaped out a Mountain Boy, and with one voice a shout went up:

"Surrender!"

It was no use resisting.

The Yorkers were outnumbered.

They were blown with the long run, while their enemies were fresh and their muskets loaded.

"To whom are we to surrender?" asked the officer.

"To Col. Allen and his Green Mountain Boys," was the answer.

"On what terms?"

"The same you gave us," answered Baker.

"Yes, you are invaders of another colony, and must be treated as marauders," added Allen.

"We are prisoners of war."

"Not any more than we were, but you bound us with cords, and you must submit to the same treatment."

"It is an outrage."

"Very likely you think so, but you should do to others as you would they should do to you. The example was set by you, not me."

Turning to his men, Allen ordered them to convey the prisoners to the camp by the lake, and added:

"Shoot anyone who attempts to escape."

The order was unnecessary, for the Yorkers were too much frightened to think of escaping.

When the camp was reached Ethan Allen gave orders for the Garvans, father and son, to be arrested and brought to the camp.

Peleg Sunderland told how the rescue had been accomplished, but when he gave Zeb's version of the affair Allen shook his head and told his friends of the arch treachery of the elder Garvan, whatever his son might say to the contrary.

Before morning Zeke Garvan and his hopeful son, Zeb, were prisoners at the camp of the Mountain Boys.

Zeke expected to be shot, and whimpered like a child.

His son, Zeb, was brave, and showed that death had no terrors for him.

There was a sort of bulldog courage about him which won the admiration of even his enemies. He faced the Mountain Boys with a defiance which seemed to mean:

"What are you going to do about it?"

When Allen asked him why he had been so treacherous, he laughed as though the question was a good joke.

"I worsted the enemy, didn't I?"

"What do you mean?"

Zeb screwed up his mouth as though about to whistle, then suddenly changed and burst into another laugh.

"Come, my boy, we do not make war on boys, so tell me your motive."

"Shall I?"

"It will be for your advantage, and your father ——"

"Don't mention him. Let every tub stand on its own bottom, my father always taught me. Talk about me, if you like, but leave dad alone."

"Then, for your own sake, tell me why you did it. Did others prompt you?"

"I don't know what you mean by prompt, but if you mean did anyone tell me to do it, I say no. I thought of it all by myself, and I made a bargain with father, which he didn't keep; but he was a long time before he saw it as I did."

"Tell all your story, and leave the rest to me."

"Well, you see, father wanted money ——"

"Ah! so money stands before country?"

"Let me tell my story."

"Go on, I will not interrupt you again."

"You had better not if you want to hear what I have to say. I said father wanted money, and as the Yorkers wanted you, and offered a big sum of good money for your capture, why, I suggested to father that he get the reward. Now, don't wince; wait until you have heard all. So I got father to agree, and then you were invited to supper. I had gone for the soldiers, and there you were trapped as nicely as any bear in the mountains. Well, when you were secured I put up dad to ask when he would get the reward, and he was told he would have to go to Albany for it, and I found that he could get the reward even if you were rescued, so I wanted to make myself solid with the boys, and I came and told them which way you would be taken, and how to rescue you. So if you will let us go we shall get the reward, but the Yorkers won't get you."

Zeb spoke with such a feeling of exultation that Allen had to laugh.

"So you tried to please both parties?"

"Well, yes; but if ye don't get the money we shan't be pleased with the result."

"Have you told me the truth?"

"Of course I have, and I am itching to get the reward so that I may laugh at the enemy."

"And try to play the same prank again."

"No, I want to join you; I am tired of home. My, won't the Yorkers be mad at having to pay the money and not get you anyway?"

"They will not pay the reward."

"Then I'll fight until they do."

Allen called a council of the boys and asked what should be done with the prisoners.

"Hang them all, every one of them," was the advice of Peleg Sunderland.

"I say, keep them as hostages, and if any of our men are caught, deal with the Yorkers as they deal with our men," said Baker.

"And I think," remarked Allen, slowly and with great deliberation, "that we ought to liberate the soldiers, who only did as they were ordered, and punish Farmer Garvan."

"Let us leave the whole matter to the colonel."

"Good! he is always right."

This course was adopted, and Allen accepted the trust.

He ordered the soldiers to be brought before him, and then addressed them, telling them how some had counseled hanging, but as they were fellow-Americans it was resolved to liberate them, because they had only obeyed orders.

He expressed a wish that they would go back to their own colony and tell the Yorkers that the men of the mountains would never give up their lands while one of them remained alive.

The officer in charge spoke for his men.

He thanked Allen for his merciful conduct, and declared that the duty had been distasteful, but that as soldiers they must act without question.

After the Yorkers left the camp, Allen ordered the farmer to be brought before him.

"Farmer Garvan," he said, "you have been guilty of the greatest crime it is possible for a man to commit. You offered hospitality, and then, like Judas, you betrayed those who trusted you. Your offense is worse, seeing that you are a grantee of New Hampshire. By all the laws of war you ought to be hanged — —"

"Spare me!" whined the farmer.

"You did not spare me, but for the sake of a little money would have condemned me to death. You are a coward, or you would meet your fate boldly. A man who risks so much should not cry out for mercy when his rascality fails. I will not hang you — —"

"Thank you. Heaven — —"

"Stay! Do not call Heaven into a defense of treachery. I order that you be stripped and receive one hundred lashes on the bare back, such punishment to be meted out to you in accordance with the laws laid down by the convention at Bennington."

Garvan fell on his knees and with uplifted hands prayed for mercy.

"It will kill me, I know it will. Oh, spare me, and I will serve you, I——"

"Each of my men will give you a stroke with a good, strong oaken or beechen stick, and may the punishment teach you that treachery never pays."

In vain the man cried for mercy.

Allen could never forgive treachery.

The Green Mountain Boys hurried to cut sticks from the trees which grew by the lake, and each submitted his stick to Allen, who rejected quite a number because they were too large.

Zeke was stripped and tied to a tree, his hands above his head. The first man was called to administer his stroke, when Zeb, who had been standing, listening to the decision, rushed forward, and placing himself between his father and the mountaineer, said:

"Strike, but not father. Let me bear the punishment, for it was all my fault, it was all my doing."

"Stand aside."

"I will not."

"Drag him away," commanded Baker.

Two of the mountaineers stepped up to the boy, who had clasped his arms around his father's waist.

He held on so tightly that to drag him away they must hurt him.

Baker ordered the men to whip him until he loosed his grasp, but Allen stopped the execution of this order.

"Stop! Boy, you have won. I thought you were bad at heart, but I see you love your father, and for your sake I remit the punishment."

Zeb fell on his knees and clasped Allen's legs.

"Bless you! If anyone ever says a word against you in my hearing he shall die, that he shall."

"Release the prisoner."

When Zeke was free Allen ordered him to give up the paper signed by the soldiers.

"And lose my reward?"

"Yes; I will not allow you to be rewarded for treachery."

Garvan had no option in the matter, and so he gave up the document, which certified that he was entitled to the reward for the capture of Ethan Allen and Remember Baker.

Zeb pleaded hard to be allowed to join the Mountain Boys, and Allen consented provisionally that he should stay in the camp and hold no conversation with his old companions.

"I am afraid you acted foolishly," said Baker. "Others will follow the farmer's example."

"I think not. Mercy never yet failed; sternness often leads to disaster. I am satisfied with what has been done."

In this, as in many other instances, Ethan Allen, rebel though he was called, outlaw as he was decreed to be, showed the largeness of his heart.

"We shall have to break camp. It is possible others besides those who have been liberated will know of our nearness and profit by it."

"Where shall we go, colonel?"

"To Middlebury. We will not secrete ourselves, but openly show that we are in the field to oppose New York in its pretensions."

CHAPTER XII.
THE OPENING OF THE WAR.

The people of Middlebury welcomed Allen and his Green Mountain Boys with enthusiasm.

They knew that their only chance of maintaining their lands—lands which they had reclaimed and made valuable—was by assisting Allen in his crusade against the pretensions of New York.

Success perched upon his banner, and not only was he able to hold the lands for the people, but he drove the New York settlers out of the district.

He had drafted a petition to the English king, asking that Vermont should be a separate colony, having its own governor and its legislature.

But before that petition reached England the revolution had broken out.

The Boston Port bill had been passed, which enacted that no kind of merchandise should any longer be shipped or landed at the wharves of Boston.

The custom house was removed to Salem, but the people of that town refused the honor conferred on them by the tyrant who ruled the destinies of England and the colonies.

The inhabitants of Marblehead offered the free use of their warehouses to the merchants of Boston. The Colonial Assembly stood by the people.

Then England passed an act of parliament annuling the charter of Massachusetts. The people were declared rebels, and the governor was ordered to send to England for trial all persons who should resist the royal officers.

A colonial congress was called to assemble at Philadelphia. Eleven colonies were represented, and it was unanimously agreed to sustain Massachusetts in her conflict with parliament.

An address was sent to King George, another to the English nation, and a third to the people of Canada.

As soon as England received the addresses an order was made by which the governor was directed to reduce the colonists by force.

So we see that England took the initiative in the war which was to deprive her of her richest colonies.

A fleet and an army of ten thousand men were sent to America to aid in the work of subjugation.

Gov. Gage seized Boston Neck and fortified it. The military stores in the arsenals of Cambridge and Charlestown were conveyed to Boston, and the general assembly was ordered to disband.

Instead of accepting their dismissal, the members resolved themselves into a provincial congress, and voted to equip an army of twelve thousand men to defend the colony.

As soon as the people of Boston learned the intentions of the governor, they concealed their ammunition in carts of rubbish and conveyed it to Concord, sixteen miles away.

The wrath of the governor was especially directed against Samuel Adams and John Hancock, who were looked upon as the leaders of the rebellion.

An expedition was sent against Concord, and eight hundred men marched toward the town.

But the people of Boston were not to be taken by surprise.

Bells were rung and cannon fired, and the citizens were informed of the expedition.

Joseph Warren—all honor to him—had dispatched Paul Revere and William Dawes to ride with all speed to Concord and Lexington and rouse the whole country to resistance.

A company of one hundred and thirty Minute Men assembled on Lexington Common and awaited the approach of the enemy, but after staying some hours they dispersed.

At five o'clock in the morning the English appeared, led by the notorious Pitcairn.

The Minute Men had gone back to their homes, tired of waiting; but seventy, led by Capt. Parker, were roused and reached the common before the enemy.

Pitcairn rode up to them and exclaimed:

"Disperse, you villains! Throw down your arms, ye rebels, and disperse!"

The Minute Men stood defiant and still.

Pitcairn discharged his pistol at them and shouted to his men:

"Fire!"

The first volley whistled through the air, and sixteen of the Minute Men fell, dead or wounded.

The rest fired a few random shots and dispersed.

The English pressed on to Concord.

The people had quietly removed most of the ammunition, and the English found but little worth taking. They started to sack the town.

While they were doing this the Minute Men had rallied and began to assemble from all quarters.

A company of English guarded the bridge over Concord River. They were attacked by the Minute Men and two English soldiers were killed. The Minute Men captured the bridge, and the enemy began a retreat into the town, and then on the road to Lexington.

On every side the patriots assembled. For six miles the battle waged.

Every tree, every house and barn sheltered the patriots, who poured a murderous fire into the ranks of the retreating English.

Had it not been for the arrival of reinforcements under Lord Percy, the English army would have been completely routed.

The fight continued right up to Charlestown, and only ceased because the people feared the fleet would burn the city.

The first battle had been fought.

The English had suffered a loss of two hundred and seventy-three, while the patriots lost only eighty-three in dead and wounded.

The battle of Lexington fired the country.

Within a few days an army of twenty thousand men had gathered round Boston.

New Hampshire sent its militia, with John Stark at its head; Rhode Island sent her quota under the leadership of Nathaniel Greene.

New Haven was not behind, for a regiment was dispatched from that city with Benedict Arnold as leader.

All this news was conveyed to Ethan Allen by Eben Pike, who had been dispatched on the dangerous mission to Boston to find out what the Provincials meant to do. No more trusty messenger could have been found than the young scout of the Green Mountains.

"What shall we do?" asked Baker.

"Fight!" was Allen's curt reply.

"Shall we join the patriots at Boston?"

"No; Connecticut has offered a thousand dollars toward the expenses of capturing Ticonderoga, and that reward we will win."

To capture the fort with its treasures would be to strike a blow at England's supremacy which would tell more than any concerted action at Boston.

"Call the roll," ordered Allen.

Two hundred and seventy men answered the call, and Allen shouted for joy.

"Men of the Great Mountains, we are strong, because a mountain boy is worth ten men of the valleys. We shall capture Ticonderoga. I cannot offer you life; many may be killed, more wounded; but remember we have fought for our homes, we must now fight for our country. We have driven the Yorkers out of the Green Mountains, we must now drive the English out of America, or compel them to recognize our right to govern ourselves. Will you follow me?"

A tremendous shout in the affirmative went up from those brave patriots, and Ethan Allen was so overcome with emotion that for a few moments he could not speak.

Then, raising his sword above his head, he shouted:

"On to Ticonderoga! Victory and freedom, or death, for every man who hears my voice!"

And the Green Mountain Boys took up the cry:

"On to Ticonderoga! Victory or death!"

CHAPTER XIII.
BENEDICT ARNOLD.

"At last I see my way to a position. They said I was a ne'er-do-well. We shall see!"

The speaker, a fine, handsome-looking man, paced the floor of a small room in Cambridge.

It was one week after the battle of Lexington.

He was restless; every muscle in his body seemed to quiver with excitement.

Anyone looking at him would prefer him as a friend rather than an enemy, for there was that in his face which betokened strong passion.

He was ambitious. For the gratification of that ambition he would sacrifice anything, even honor.

He had been brought up as a merchant, and had splendid opportunities in his native Colony of Connecticut for success, but he was restless, and wanted a fame greater than he could obtain as a merchant.

He had suggested the formation of a company of militia, to be called the "Governor's Guards," and had also hinted that they should rival the royal guards of England in appearance and attire.

The governor was pleased with the suggestion, for he loved display, and commissioned Benedict Arnold to put into effect his suggestion, and to take the rank of captain.

Arnold cared less for the career of a merchant than ever.

He designed a uniform which should outshine even the famous Life Guards of London in splendor.

Buckling on a sword, he would pose before a mirror and salute his own reflected image in the glass.

Gathering around him a number of well-connected young men, men of good figure and tall in stature, he proceeded to impress upon them his own importance, and made them believe that all the honor of their position depended upon his favor.

Arnold was a favorite, and so the young men of New Haven accepted his authority and became the willing followers of Capt. Arnold.

The governor threw a wet blanket on his scheme when he told him that if the guards wanted uniforms they must purchase them, for the funds of the colony could not be used for such a purpose.

Arnold had to moderate his gorgeousness and accept a much plainer uniform for his guards.

The company was formed, and drill commenced. The young captain showed that he knew more about the manual of arms than he did of mercantile practices.

The militia grumbled at the harshness of the discipline, but a few words from their captain won them over.

When the war commenced Arnold was a strong royalist, or tory.

He wanted the guards to be recognized by England as a part of the royal forces. In fancy he saw himself driving the "rebels" into the sound and being sent for to London to receive the thanks of the king in person; he imagined himself promoted to the rank of general, and perhaps made life governor of one of the colonies.

But the airy castles he built fell to the ground when he was bluntly told that the king could do without his "guards," and that when there was need of soldiers the king could provide them.

From that moment Arnold resolved on throwing in his lot with the very men he had asked permission to shoot down. He became a "rebel."

When the news of the battle of Lexington reached New Haven he clapped his hands and became more excited than he had ever known himself to be.

He called his guards together, and in an impassioned speech bade them be ready to march against the English, and win freedom for their native land and honor and renown for themselves.

He denounced the king.

He ridiculed the parliament.

The tories were treated to such an outburst of eloquent denunciation that, had any of them heard him, they would have trembled.

"Guards! soldiers of the nation! I salute you. To you is intrusted a banner which must ever be kept in the front of the battle. Some of us may fall, but, if we do, our names shall be writ on our country's history in imperishable letters. To those who survive no honor will be begrudged, no reward will be too ample for a proud country to bestow.

"We shall meet the foe. We shall cross swords with the hirelings of a tyrant. Our arms will be triumphant, for justice is with us, and God will bless our swords. To-morrow we march to Massachusetts, to join our brothers there, and all the world shall ring with the doings of the Governor's Guards of Connecticut."

He fired his men with enthusiasm, and they were ready to follow him to death, if need be.

Arrived at Cambridge, he was received warmly, but so was John Stark and his New Hampshire militia, and equally well did he find the men of Massachusetts greet Nathaniel Greene and his militia from Rhode Island.

Arnold had expected a greater enthusiasm. In his heart he had fancied himself appointed general of the army of the Provincials, and therefore he was hurt when he learned that he was only one among many.

"The king insulted me," he said, as he paced the floor, "the tories did not care for me, and now these Provincials treat me as if I were one of them, instead of being— — Well, what is it, Eli?"

Sergt. Eli Forest, of the Governor's Guards, entered the room.

"Captain, I have just heard that one Ethan Allen has undertaken to capture Ticonderoga, for which our governor has offered a thousand dollars for expenses."

"Well?"

"Would it not be well for us to join with Col. Allen— —"

"Eh?"

"Do not think me rash, captain, but you have given me permission to speak as I think."

"So I have, Eli, and for the sake of our old college days and the good times we shared, you can always speak your mind to me."

"Then, captain, I thought that this man, Allen, knew nothing of fighting save a sheriff's posse, and you could become the general and lead the men to Ticonderoga and then to Crown Point, and who knows, you might drive the English back into Canada, and, joining with the French, compel England to sue for peace, and you could name your own terms."

"Talk, talk, talk! How easy it is to talk, Eli, but how different is action. Go; when I have thought over your suggestion I will let you know my decision."

Eli Forest had the most implicit confidence in Benedict Arnold. As boys they had gone to the same school, and when they left school they entered college and graduated at the same time. During all those years Eli had always looked upon Arnold as a superior being. When the men were enrolled as guards Eli felt that the height of his ambition was reached, for, with Arnold as captain, the guards would rival any military body in the country.

Arnold was as fond of his friend as he could be of anyone; he gave him greater freedom of speech, and listened to him when others would have been treated very cavalierly.

When Benedict Arnold was alone he showed by every line on his face how pleased he was with the suggestion made by his old-time friend.

"It is the opportunity of my life. What does Ethan Allen know about war? He is a country farmer, and can fight a sheriff's posse, and perhaps a few soldiers in his mountains; but to take Ticonderoga? Bah! He will fail unless I help him, and then the glory shall be mine."

Arnold walked quickly up and down the floor, his hands clinched, his face lighted up with ambitious fire.

"Yes, the glory shall be mine," he continued, "and once let me have Ticonderoga and Crown Point, and then — — Ah! what then?"

He crossed to the window and looked out.

John Stark was marching past at the head of his sturdy New Hampshire boys, and the people cheered.

"If I hold Lake Champlain and the Green Mountains I can dictate my own terms. I shall hold the key to the situation. Canada can be mine, and Massachusetts will be glad to make terms with me. If I fail to make good terms with the colonies I can go to England and say: 'You will be driven out of America unless I say stay, and I shall not say that unless you give me——' Well, what now?"

The orderly entered and told Arnold that he was wanted at the headquarters of the Provincial army at once.

"Tell the council that I—will not—— I mean I will not delay."

Once more alone, he showed his restlessness.

"They order me—me!—Capt. Benedict Arnold! Well, let me join Allen and his Green Mountain Boys, and I shall do the ordering, or my star has dimmed its luster."

One hour later he called together his guards and told them that they were to be ready to march at a moment's notice.

"A soldier's first lesson is that of obedience," he said to them, "and I am going to try you in many ways. In the expedition we are about to undertake I shall only be of the same rank as yourselves. Obey whoever may be your commander, but be ready to accept me as your leader at any time."

Eli, on behalf of the guards, promised that whatever Arnold might order it would be their pleasure to obey.

"Sergt. Eli Forest, stand forward."

Eli obeyed and saluted.

"Lieut. Percival has obtained leave of absence. He will join the army in Cambridge when that leave expires. The grade of lieutenant is an important one, and I appoint you, Eli Forest, first lieutenant of the Governor's Guards."

Eli thanked his chief for the new honor, and Arnold had bound him still closer to him.

CHAPTER XIV.
ARNOLD'S POWERS OF FASCINATION.

"On the choice of friends
Our good or evil name depends."

"Colonel, a number of armed men are marching this way, and I like not their appearance," said the young Eben Pike, hurriedly and with gasping breath, as he entered the presence of Ethan Allen.

"They most likely are friends, Eben."

"They may be, colonel, but I thought you ought to know."

"You acted wisely, as you usually do. Did you meet Mistress Baker?"

"Yes, colonel, and a fair young maiden she is. I wish I had a sister like her."

Allen laughed and looked at the boy, whose face was a brighter color than usual.

"You will learn to like some one else's sister better than your own, if you had one."

Eben blushed still more and was about to leave when the colonel made him send Baker at once.

Remember Baker had a sister, pretty and winsome. She had been visiting for a year in New Haven, and decided to return to her brother's home at the very time he was on the march with Allen.

Baker had an aunt living near Lake Champlain, and he decided to place Martha with her. Good friends escorted Martha to a place a few miles from where the Mountain Boys were to camp prior to their attack on Fort Ticonderoga, and Eben was dispatched to escort the young maiden to her brother. Eben had fulfilled the task and wished the distance had been several times as far; but a few miles from the camp he had seen the regiment of guards on the march, and at once thought it his duty to report.

Remember Baker entered the presence of Ethan Allen and listened to the story told by Eben.

"Martha saw them," said Baker, "and she declared that their leader was a man who was noted for being a great loyalist in New Haven."

"So! Let all the men be ready in case of emergency, and do you see that they are well prepared for attack!"

"I shall see to it."

"Does Mistress Martha feel tired after her long journey?"

"No; she very naively says that she was tired until she was met by Eben, and from that time her weariness ceased."

"Natural, very. Eben felt that way also, and his face was as red as a turkey gobbler's comb when he entered here."

In less than an hour Lieut. Eli Forest approached the camp, bearing a white flag.

He asked to be admitted to the presence of Ethan Allen.

"Col. Allen, this gentleman craves an interview."

"Capt. Baker, I shall be pleased to confer with him."

Eli was rather surprised at the courtesy shown by Ethan and Baker to each other. He had been led to believe the Mountain Boys to be a lot of uneducated, boorish farmers.

He, a college graduate, knew that he was in the presence of his equals.

"I am commissioned by my superior, Col. Arnold, to ask you to favor him with an audience."

"Might I ask who I am speaking with?"

"I have the honor to be lieutenant of the Connecticut Guards. I am Eli Forest."

"Tell Col. Arnold that I shall be pleased to see him, and, believe me, I am proud to have met Lieut. Forest."

When Forest returned to Arnold he found the New Haven colonel very anxious.

"Well, what says the farmer?"

"He may be a farmer, but he is a well-educated gentleman."

"You don't mean——"

"We have been deceived. You will find that he is our—my equal."

"So much the better; I shall win the surer."

In the camp of the mountaineers the center of attraction was Martha Baker. Many of the Bennington boys knew her, though she had greatly improved during her stay at New Haven.

She sought the presence of Col. Allen and besought him to be careful of his treatment of the guardsman of New Haven.

"If it is Benedict Arnold who is coming, he means you no good," she said, very earnestly; "my friend in New Haven knew him well, and she was certain that he was in favor of England."

"Thank you, Martha; I will know how to deal with him. I am glad that you have told me."

Benedict Arnold lost no time in seeking an audience with Ethan Allen.

"I have come from Cambridge," he said, "with but one object in view."

"I shall be very pleased to hear your project, if you care to confide it to me."

"I heard of your fame"—Ethan bowed—"and I felt that if there was to be any great work accomplished, Col. Ethan Allen was the man to make it apparent."

Arnold had spoken with great deference. "I was appointed colonel by the Provincial Council; but when I heard that Ethan Allen and his Green Mountain Boys were about to attack Fort Ticonderoga, I thought that I could serve my country best by offering myself and my guards to him, and I ask no other favor than to be allowed to enlist under your banner as a private soldier."

"My dear colonel, I cannot think of such a thing."

"On no other terms would I consent. My men are all well drilled and are ready to join you under the same conditions."

"Let us meet on equal terms; we will jointly command."

"No, Col. Allen; in military matters there should be no divided authority. I will serve under you, and if you wish my advice I shall be ready to give it, but I will not accept a share in the command."

The interview was a long one.

Ethan Allen was completely fascinated with Arnold. He believed that if there was a genuine patriot in the colony it was he.

Arnold, having recovered from his surprise at finding Allen an educated man, conceived a liking for him and resolved to act squarely in all his dealings with him.

Arnold was better read in history than the mountaineer, and he knew the history of Ticonderoga as well as he knew the later history of New Haven.

"The French knew what they were doing when they fortified Ticonderoga," Arnold remarked, when the strength of the fort was being discussed.

"Tell me all you know about it, will you not?"

"My dear Allen, I am always at your service. You remember—but no, you would be too young; we were but boys then—but in 1755 Gen. William Johnson was ordered by the British to drive the French from the shores of Lake Champlain. Johnson had a fine body of men, three thousand four hundred in number, including a body of friendly Mohawks. Oh, those Mohawks! They are fighters, every one of them. I wish we had a thousand of them with us."

"We do not need them."

"No, but we shall before the English are taught the lesson we intend to teach them—that is, to mind their own business. The French general, Dieskau, who was commandant at Crown Point, was one of the most daring men of whom I have ever heard. He had only fourteen hundred men, French, Indians and Canadians, all told, but with this force he made up his mind he would anticipate the movements of the English and drive them back to Albany. He sailed up the lake to South Bay. From there he marched to the upper springs of Wood Creek, intending to pass the English army and capture Fort Edward before the alarm could be given. But the news was carried to Gen. Johnson. A natural, a boy, half an idiot, ran into the general's presence and cried out: 'The French are marching like mad!' A scout was sent out and the truth learned. Col. Williams, with a force of a thousand men, accompanied by Mohawk Chief

Hendrick, with two hundred warriors, set out to relieve the threatened fort."

"Hendrick was a very old man, was he not?"

"Yes, he was gray-headed, and though very old he was as stalwart as any of the younger men of the tribe. Dieskau had been misled as to the route, and found himself four miles to the north of Fort Edward, when he should have been there. His scouts reported that Williams and Hendrick were marching to the fort, and the daring Frenchman quickly ordered his forces into ambush, and the English were entrapped. Both Williams and Hendrick fell dead, and the English were badly routed. Johnson heard the noise of battle and quickly extemporized breastworks by felling trees; the cannon were brought into position and then the English awaited the triumphant French. It must have been a glorious fight.

"The Indians, with Dieskau, when they saw the cannon, quietly walked to a hill at a safe distance, and watched the battle. The Canadians, who had hoped the Indians would have done the most of the fighting, were disheartened and left the French to make the onset alone. Bravely they fought, and for five hours, the battle raged. Johnson was wounded early in the tight, and the men fought without a leader."

"But Johnson got the credit?"

"Yes, and was made a baronet by England; but, between you and I, the man was only slightly wounded, and was glad of an excuse to escape the danger of the battle."

"Johnson was no coward."

"Perhaps not; but have you not heard of that commander who, when wounded, insisted on staying on the field and giving orders until he dropped dead? That was a true hero, if you like. Then note the difference. Dieskau was wounded three times and would not retire. He sat on a tree stump and refused to be carried off the field. A renegade Frenchman who had joined the English went up to him to make him a prisoner. Dieskau was about to hand the man his watch as a token of surrender, but the Frenchman, thinking the general intended to draw a pistol, fired, and the brave commander dropped, mortally wounded. But though the victory was with the English, it was dearly purchased. The French were not disheartened, for they reinforced Crown Point and seized Ticonderoga, which they fortified."

"Is Ticonderoga so very strong?" asked Allen, who had listened so attentively to the historical narrative told by Arnold.

"Yes. Abercrombie for four hours stormed it. Column after column dashed with great bravery against the breastworks, but only to meet with failure. Abercrombie could have returned with a larger army and heavier guns, but he did not. He had fifteen thousand men, while the French had not more than eight thousand on the outside. In 1759 the French, being hard pressed, dismantled the fort and the English walked into it. It cost the English eight million pounds to repair, enlarge and strengthen it."

"And in a few days it will be in our possession."

"I hope so."

"It must be."

"Have you sent out any scouts to find its strength?"

"Yes, one—a boy named Ebenezer Pike."

"A boy?"

"Yes, a boy that I would back against all the men I ever saw."

"He may betray you."

"Col. Arnold, that makes three times you have expressed a fear of some one betraying our cause. Do not do it again, or I may — —"

Allen paused. He did not wish to give offense.

"What? Speak out, man!"

"I may doubt you. I always was taught to think that a suspicious person was to be feared."

"Ha, ha, ha! Allen, do you see that sun?"

"Of course."

"It shines for all?"

"Yes."

"It is always constant? It never refuses to shine?"

"No."

"Then do not doubt me until that sun ceases to be constant and true."

CHAPTER XV.
THE HERO OF TICONDEROGA.

Arnold appeared to agree with every suggestion made by Allen, and no man could be more pleasant.

Not one atom of distrust of Arnold was to be found in the whole of the mountaineer's mind.

Certainly he had no reason for it save the strong distrust manifested by Remember Baker because of the stories Martha had brought from New Haven.

On the evening of the ninth of May the combined forces of Allen and Arnold appeared on the eastern shore of Lake Champlain, opposite Ticonderoga.

The march had been so well planned and executed that the English had no knowledge of the movement of the Mountain Boys.

A difficulty, which had not been foreseen, had to be overcome.

There were only three small boats in which the men could be conveyed across the lake.

Usually there was quite a fleet of boats there, but the soldiers had taken most of the boats farther up the lake.

Arnold suggested the construction of rafts, but the felling of trees might make so much noise that the attention of the garrison might be called to it and the whole plan fail.

Men were sent up the shore to search for boats, while others were instructed to look for anything which could be utilized for rafts.

Half the night was wasted in the vain search, and some of the boys were discouraged.

Allen called the leaders together and asked the simple question:

"What shall we do?"

Let it not be thought that he hesitated. No, Ethan Allen never did that; he knew just what would be best, but he also knew that the men were more confident if they were consulted.

Eli Forest was the first to answer.

"It is impossible for us to cross, so I think it would be best to retire into the woods and fell trees, so that we might fashion rafts."

"How long would that delay us?"

"Not more than a week."

"What say you, Baker?"

"I do not like delay, yet—Ticonderoga is strong, and ten men could hold the place against a hundred."

"And you, Col. Arnold?"

"I am a soldier, and am ready to follow my superior. What he orders I shall loyally help to carry out."

"We will all do that," said Baker, half ashamed that he had shown any shadow of doubt about the advisability of attacking the fort.

"I know you are all true soldiers," replied Allen, "and I am ready to lead you against the fort. I think we can breakfast on the rations England has provided."

"Lead on and we will follow."

"Forest, do you pick the men in your company who have the strongest nerves and the pluckiest spirits to cross first; take the largest of the two large boats and get as many of the men over as possible."

"It shall be done."

"And you, Baker, follow the same instruction in reference to the Mountain Boys. The small boat we will reserve for Col. Arnold and myself. When you reach the other side, remember that there must not be a sound. No word must be uttered, no fire made, but let every man lie in the long grass and wait for orders."

A crew was selected for each boat, and the work of transporting the little army across the lake was commenced.

The men pulled steadily and noiselessly across the waters of the beautiful lake which the Indians called "Troquois," and the early French settlers, who objected to honoring the explorer, Samuel de Champlain, "Mere les Iroquois," and still later, "Iracosia."

It was slow work, and the men asked permission to swim across, but Allen was afraid the swim would be too exhausting.

When day broke the work had to cease, for the men at the fort would have seen the boats and been put on their guard.

Arnold looked at the handful of men and predicted failure.

Allen counted the men and found eighty-three.

That was the strength of his little army.

It seemed absurd to think of attacking one of the strongest fortresses on the continent with such a handful of men.

True, the garrison was small, but it was intrenched behind strong walls, a well-filled moat and a line of breastworks carefully designed, and improved bastions.

Allen called all his men together and addressed them.

"It is for your country that you will risk your lives," he said, "and while you take care not to run into needless danger, remember that only the daring will succeed. If we enter the fort, as we shall undoubtedly do, set up a shout which shall make the garrison think we have eight hundred instead of eighty men. Be brave, and the victory will be ours."

A thrill of excitement made every heart beat fast; cheeks glowed with pleasure, heads were borne erect with pride, and the few men looked invincible.

Allen and Arnold led the way; they never were in the rear.

When close to the fort they made a dash and gained the gateway.

"Stand back!" exclaimed the sentry.

He raised his musket to fire, but Allen knocked it on one side.

"Are you mad? Do you want to die?" he asked.

"Better die than be craven," answered the English soldier, bravely.

Allen had seized him round the waist and thrown him to the floor; he picked himself up and ran into the fort, closely followed by the mountaineers.

Suddenly the Green Mountain Boys set up such a shout as few garrisons had ever heard.

"We are inside," said Baker, exultingly.

"Ay, but not out," answered Forest, rather gloomily.

"Form into line!" shouted Arnold.

The men formed, facing the barracks, and were ready to fire should the garrison show fight.

Allen left the command of the men in the hands of Arnold, while he rushed to the quarters of the commandant.

Capt. Delaplace was asleep.

He had not heard the shout, though it was loud enough to wake the dead almost.

A sentinel stood guard outside the commandant's door.

Allen placed a pistol at his head and ordered him to stand aside.

The man obeyed like one in a dream.

Allen stood by the bedside of the sleeping commandant.

"Get up!" shouted the mountaineer.

The voice was loud enough to rouse the sleeper, who thought that the French had taken a fancy to come down the lake and try to recapture the fortress.

"Get up!"

The commandant sat up in bed.

"What do you want? Who are you?"

"Surrender this fortress instantly."

"By what authority?"

Allen flourished his sword as he replied:

"In the name of the Great Jehovah and the Continental Congress!"

Delaplace did not hesitate.

A sword was in close proximity to his heart, the shouts of the men outside showed that the enemy was in possession of the fort, so what could he do but surrender?

He reached to the side of the bed and took his sword.

"There is my sword, sir. I trust that you will allow me to dress."

"Certainly; report to me in half an hour. Sorry to disturb your sleep, captain, but war, you know, is not always considerate."

The English flag was borne on the breeze, and floated proudly over the fort.

Allen looked up at it and sighed.

It was a gallant flag, and a brave man does not like to see a flag of a great nation humiliated, even though he is fighting against it.

"Haul down the flag!"

"What shall we run up, colonel?"

The Provincials had no flag, and Allen ordered the English flag to be again run up, but with the Union down.

Across the waters of the lake the men were watching, and when they saw the flag run up, with the Union down, they knew that the fort had been taken, and they set up a cheer that could be heard across the water.

A hundred and twenty cannon and a vast amount of military stores fell into the hands of the Americans.

Great Britain had expended forty million dollars on Fort Ticonderoga from first to last, and a few undisciplined Mountain Boys wrested this proud possession from her.

Boats brought over the rest of the combined forces of Arnold and Allen, and the leader of the mountaineers made good his promise that they should breakfast in the fort on rations paid for by their enemy.

When an inventory had been made and sent in duplicate to the assembly of Connecticut and of Massachusetts by trusty messengers, Allen called together his officers and thrilled them by declaring that their work had only just begun.

"To-day we have captured the strongest fortress in America; in two days more we must be in Crown Point."

"And again we pledge ourselves to the hero of Ticonderoga, who will lead us to triumph!" exclaimed Baker.

"Ay, and our cry shall be," echoed Forest, "Liberty Freedom and Independence!"

CHAPTER XVI.
THE TEMPTATION.

Capt. Delaplace was fretful and soured by his defeat.

"If it had been in open fight," he said, "I should not have cared so much; but to be caught in a trap, it is enough to make a man kill himself."

He was speaking to Benedict Arnold, and that patriot was ready to listen almost gloatingly to the story.

Arnold was a peculiar man; he was kind and sympathetic, yet was ready to rejoice over the sufferings of the fallen.

Allen had asked Arnold to spend a portion of the day with the defeated officer, so that he might be more consoled, for company is always soothing.

Delaplace was a diplomat; he had imbibed the idea that every man had his price; in other words, that every man could be influenced for or against a cause by bribery in some form or other.

Being a quick reader of character, he saw that Arnold was ambitious, and he at once began to wonder whether ambition would lead him to be false to Allen.

"You have treated me very kindly," he said to Arnold, "and I shall report to my superiors, though — —"

He paused, and there was a world of meaning in that sudden silence.

"Why do you hesitate? I know what you would say."

"Do you?"

"Yes; shall I tell you?"

"If you please."

"And you will tell me whether I am right?"

"On my honor as a soldier and a gentleman."

"You were about to say that such a recommendation would not even be a plea in mitigation of the death penalty if I should fall into the hands of the English."

Again there was silence.

"I am answered. Your silence proves that I am right. You need not think I am offended. I know I should be treated as a rebel, not as a prisoner of war."

"And, knowing this, you joined these men against the rule of your sovereign?"

"I knew that if the colonists failed the leaders would be hanged; if they succeeded they would found a new nation, and the chances were worth risking."

"Did you not think that England has a large army and a strong navy at her back?"

"Yes, and I knew it had strong forts; this is one of them."

"You sneer! I admit that England behaved scurvily in allowing me to have so few men."

"Nay, nay, captain. Fifty men, if they felt an interest in their work, could hold this fort against an army."

"You are the victor and so have a right to rebuke me. But do not think England will allow the colonies to be independent."

"Perhaps not, but at any rate the colonies will have won respect for themselves."

"But the leaders will be hanged."

"So let it be."

"Can you face the thought of death like that?"

"I can, for my country will be saved from a serfdom which no self-respecting nation should submit to."

"If—mind, I say if, for I do not think there is the remotest chance—but if the colonies were successful, what could they do for you? I suppose you might be a governor, or something like that, with no salary to speak of, while if you had remained loyal to your king you might have a chance— —"

"Of being snubbed, insulted and laughed at."

Delaplace smiled. He had learned the cause of Arnold's action in joining the colonists—it was disappointed ambition. Could he play on that and win over Arnold? If so, then he would regain the fort, and that by treachery; but what of that? Would not the result justify the means?

"My dear general"—Arnold smiled at the title—"if anyone insulted or snubbed you it was through a misunderstanding. Tell me about it, and I think all can be rectified."

"It is too late."

"Not so; it is never too late for a great nation to rectify a wrong done to even the humblest of its subjects, let alone a man of such undoubted courage and rectitude as Gen. Arnold."

"I am not a general, but only a captain—in this adventure only a private."

"You should be a general. If the king knew you as well as I have learned to do in these few hours, you most likely would have the control of the army in the colonies."

"But the king will never have an opportunity to know me."

"Why not?"

"Only success can make me known to the king."

"Or failure; and then it would be too late."

"You see how impossible it would be for the king to know me."

"If I speak confidentially will you treat it as sacred to you alone?"

"Certainly."

"Pledge me your honor that you will never divulge what I am going to say."

"I am a soldier and a gentleman. My word is enough."

"Then I will accept your word. If I were free I could gain the ear of the king's advisers."

"But you are not free yet, and it may be some time before an exchange can be made."

"Exchange! Do you not know that there will be no exchange possible? If any of the rebels fall into the hands of the English they will be shot or hanged at once."

"In that case you would stand a poor showing."

"How so?"

"Because the first man taken by your side and hanged would lead us to hang an equal number of your men, and officers would have the first piece of rope."

Delaplace had not expected to hear such strong sentiments from Arnold, but he laughed and said that a soldier dealing with rebels knew that he took great risks, and that he must be prepared for them.

"But," he added, in a whisper, "if I could slip out of this fort and gain the English lines — —"

"But you cannot slip out."

"If you were to help me I would guarantee that you would be a general of the English army in less than forty-eight hours, and, once gain that position, there is no limit to your success."

Arnold listened.

It was wrong of him to do so.

There was a temporary hesitation, but in a few seconds of time that passed.

"Captain, you have dishonored yourself by suggesting treason, and I have dishonored myself in listening. Know this: I have given my allegiance to the cause of the Provincials, and I will rise or fall with them."

"Be it so. I shall live to see you hanged as a rebel."

Arnold bowed very low in acknowledgment of the kindly expression of opinion.

"Thank you, Capt. Delaplace. I have no wish to see you hanged, but should the English hang even a private in our ranks, I should have no hesitation in hanging you with my own hands."

Questionable sentiments on both sides, but Arnold felt strongly at that time, and expressed himself as he thought.

He left the room and called the sergeant on guard.

"Double your guard. If Capt. Delaplace escapes I shall hold you responsible, and your neck will feel the effects of a tightened noose."

It was a blunt way of speaking, but Arnold never was very courteous to those of lesser rank.

"I hate that man," Arnold soliloquized, "and yet—well, the die is cast. I might have risen to a proud distinction had I remained loyal to the king, but I have not, and so my lot is with the colonists, and may they win, or our lives are of but little value. How could Delaplace get the ear of the king? Zounds! I believe it was only to tempt me into disloyalty to the colonies that he made the proposition."

His soliloquy was interrupted by the entrance of Eli Forest.

"Colonel, your advice is needed. Col. Allen wishes to confer with you."

"I will be with him immediately. Ah! here he is. You honor me too much, Gen. Allen."

"Nay, we are on equal footing, my dear Arnold. I wanted to consult with you about two things. We must secure Crown Point, that is a settled fact, and we must maintain our possession of this fort. Now, what shall we do with the prisoners?"

"Keep them well guarded and wait until some of our men fall into the hands of the enemy, and then act with them as they do with us."

"Perhaps that will be the wisest plan. I had thought of liberating them on parole."

"It would be madness."

"You think so?"

"I am sure of it. In the eyes of these men we are rebels and outlaws, and their parole would not prevent them from bringing the whole force of the English against us."

"You are right. Will you appoint the guard?"

"Let Forest have charge of the prisoners and the fort."

"An admirable suggestion! So it shall be done."

"Ay, Forest, and shoot anyone who attempts to leave the fort, whether friend or foe."

"You are very stern, Arnold."

"These times demand sternness."

CHAPTER XVII.
CROWN POINT.

"Colonel, an army is approaching."

Ethan Allen at once thought that a regiment of English was about to try and wrest the fort from him.

He was agreeably disappointed when he saw that the men were his own Green Mountain Boys, led by Seth Warner.

Warner had been doing good work in Vermont, and, finding it advantageous to join his chief, he had marched his men to Ticonderoga.

A warm welcome was accorded the captain and his men, and Allen at once gave the command of the operations against Crown Point to Seth Warner.

The fortifications at Crown Point were erected at a cost of ten million dollars, and up to that time had never a shot been fired from them.

Trusting to the strength of the stone barracks and the extensive earthworks, England had kept only a small force at the fort, and at the time of the capture of Ticonderoga only a sergeant and twelve men composed the garrison.

Seth Warner was delighted at the honor conferred upon him by his chief.

Ethan Allen had a reason for keeping as strong a garrison at Ticonderoga as possible, for he feared that Delaplace might try to escape and perhaps recapture the fort.

Arnold was surly. He thought that Allen had lost confidence in him, but Allen reasoned the matter with his Connecticut hero, and satisfied him that no insult was intended.

Crown Point is about eleven miles north of Ticonderoga. The town itself lies six miles away from the fort.

Seth Warner started on his march, his men highly elated at the prospect of winning renown.

When about halfway they were met by a man dressed in the garb of a monk.

He carried a crucifix and a long staff.

His hair was white, and a long beard, which reached nearly to his waist, was as white as driven snow.

Waving his staff above his head, he called to the soldiers to stop.

Warner had no great liking for monks, though he was honest enough to respect every man's religion.

"What is it you would have, good father?" asked Warner.

"In the name of the ever true and good, I crave your assistance, and, if you will grant it, I will give you my blessing, which is better than rubies and more valuable than gold."

"In what way can we assist you, good father?"

"You are soldiers of liberty. Heaven will bless your swords, and you will live to see the flag of the tyrant go down in the dust, and a flag of a free nation will float over a free people. I am not allowed to fight, or I would gird on a sword and smite me right and left until the friends of the tyrant were all beneath the sod!"

"We thank you for your patriotic exhortation, but we have a mission to fulfill and we must not loiter."

"The mission is one which will not fail; I know that you have captured the strong fort at Ticonderoga, and that you will enter within the fortifications of Crown Point, but will you assist me?"

"What would you have us do?"

"To the east of you, one mile and one hundred yards, stands a house. It is a farmhouse. Its owner is no friend of the Provincials, and has a captive whom he holds for ransom."

"A captive? Held for ransom? Explain yourself!"

"This farmer, fearing that the English might be driven out of the country and that he would lose his possessions, because he is a great worker for the enemy, did find a young girl, who was related to one of the leaders of your holy cause, and he lured her into his house and holds her as a hostage. Should the Provincials take possession of his farm, he will kill the girl, so he says, and a man's word should be believed, and therefore I did make a vow to rescue this maiden from the grasp of the ungodly and restore her to her friends."

"Where did you say the farm was?"

"Tarry not, I beseech you, but travel to the east one mile and one hundred yards, and you will come to a snake fence; cross the field and you will see a house with a number of vines growing up its sides. Then ask for Farmer Mervale, and you have the man who dares to imprison one of the maidens the Lord loves."

Warner consulted with his friends, and they agreed that it would be well to rescue the maiden.

"You will go with us?" asked Warner.

"Nay, my duty lies in another direction."

The monk started away in an opposite direction to that which he had directed the army to take, and was soon lost to sight.

Then the men began to discuss his appearance and story.

"I do not believe him," said one.

"Yet he is a religious man, and therefore his word should be believed."

"He may be a spy."

"But why should he direct us to the farm?"

"The English may be in ambush."

"Then we must go, for, being forewarned we are forearmed, and shall gain a victory."

This idea prevailed, and the Mountain Boys commenced their march to the east.

When a mile had been traversed, as near as they could guess, Warner sent a scout forward to reconnoiter.

He returned quickly and said that there was no sign of an ambush, but the snake fence was there and the vine-covered house also.

"Go forward, Letsom, and find out all you can about the farmer and his household."

The man was an excellent fellow for such a purpose, though Seth Warner expressed a wish that Eben had been there, so that he might have gone.

Letsom returned an hour later.

"Farmer Mervale is a bitter Britisher," he reported, "and told me that if any of the rebels came to his house he would know how to deal with them. I asked him what he would do, and he replied that he would ask them to dine and would poison their soup."

"The villain!"

"He further said that every rebel, as he called us, should be shot like a rat."

"He is quite strong in his views."

"Yes, and one of his farm hands told me that a mad monk had been there, and it would be a wonder if he were alive on the morrow."

"A mad monk, said he?"

"Yes, those were his words—a mad monk."

"Boys, you have heard the report; shall we beard this Britisher in his home and find out if any maiden is imprisoned by him?"

A loud shout of assent rose from the Mountain Boys, and almost before it died away the men were on the march.

Farmer Mervale was at the door, an old musket in his hand, waiting for the "rebels."

"In the name of the king, what do you want here?"

Seth Warner answered:

"In the name of the Colonial Congress I demand the surrender of this house for the purpose of a search."

"Search! for what?"

"Guns, ammunition or anything that may be useful to the cause of liberty."

"Thieves! Whoever passes this door will have to do it over my dead body."

"Farmer Mervale, we mean you no harm if you are innocent, but if you are guilty then you must bear the punishment."

"Of what do you accuse me?"

Warner was about to equivocate and say that he believed arms were secreted on the premises, but he was too open for subterfuge, so he replied:

"We charge you with abducting and imprisoning a young maiden——"

"Ah! you have seen the mad monk?"

"Answer. Have you any maiden imprisoned on your premises?"

"If I had I should deny it, and if I have not I should still say that you are impertinent and a rebel who ought to be shot down."

The farmer had his weapon pointed at Warner and was about to shoot him, when his arm was knocked up from behind and the ball passed over his intended victim's head.

Instantly the man was seized and bound.

The musket had been seized by the hired hand, who had been the cause of the farmer's intention being frustrated.

"If you will let me join you I will fight for the cause of liberty," the man said, very earnestly.

"You must report to Col. Allen at Ticonderoga."

"I will go at once."

"Better stay with us and return when we do; we can vouch for your good act."

The farmer changed his tone when he was bound and therefore helpless. He cried out for mercy, declared that all he had said was in a joking sense, and that he hoped the Provincials would win in their fight against England.

"You coward!" hissed Warner. "I have a great mind to shoot you as an example and a warning to others."

"Spare me! I am old and——"

"Old? Why, man, you cannot be forty. Search the house!"

In a few minutes the searchers returned, leading Martha Baker, who was almost too weak to stand unsupported.

"Oh, Master Warner, I am so glad you came. I think I should have died if I had stayed another day in this horrid house."

"Tell me your story, Martha."

"I was sent by my aunt to Farmer Mervale to arrange for an exchange of eggs. You see, aunt had a lot of hen's eggs and Farmer Mervale had a lot of duck's eggs, and the two wanted to exchange. When I reached here the farmer asked me my name, and then if I was any relation of Remember Baker, and I told him that I was his sister. Then he asked me to go upstairs to help count the eggs. I did so, and the farmer told me that he was going to keep me there, because if my brother attempted to do anything to his brother, who was a soldier in Ticonderoga, he would kill me. Then he tortured me by saying that he would poison some soup and invite the rebels to dinner with him, and that when they had all eaten heartily he would kill me before their eyes."

The farmer heard the girl's statement, and, instead of denying it, declared it was all a joke, which, perhaps, it was, but it was cruel, and the perpetrator of such a joke deserved punishment.

Warner ordered his men to strip the farmer to the waist and introduce him to the "birch dance," as summary punishment was called.

Fifty good, sharp strokes across the bare back with strong beechen sticks made Farmer Mervale wish he had been less fond of joking and illegally imprisoning a girl.

Martha told how she had seen the monk, and had called to him through the open window, telling him how she had been served, and also asking him to let the Mountain Boys know of her detention.

How well the eccentric monk had fulfilled his mission we have seen.

It was rather late in the afternoon when the strong fort at Crown Point was reached.

Seth Warner called to the sentinel who stood guard at the gate.

"Tell your commander that I must see him at once."

"I cannot leave my post."

"Spoken like a brave soldier. Surrender!"

"To whom?"

"To the army of the Continental Congress."

"I am a soldier of the king, and to no one else will I surrender my gun, except my superior so wills it."

"Brave soldier. I shall be under the necessity of taking the gun away from you by force."

The man fired the musket in the air.

That was a signal for the garrison to assemble.

Seeing a hundred men with Warner, the sergeant quickly raised the white flag, and so, without the shedding of a drop of blood, two of the strongest forts on Lake Champlain passed into the hands of the brave men who were fighting for the liberty of their native land.

A garrison was left in charge of Crown Point, and then Warner marched back to Ticonderoga.

Remember Baker was full of gratitude for the rescue of his sister, and would have liked to meet Farmer Mervale at that hour, for the farmer had got off too easily, he thought.

CHAPTER XVIII.
"WHO IS COMMANDER?"

Within five days of the capture of Ticonderoga, the Green Mountain Boys, under the command of Capt. Herrick, had captured Skenesborough, while another detachment under Capt. Douglass had taken Panton, a strong fort on the lake.

As the Assembly of Connecticut had authorized the capture of Fort Ticonderoga, Allen dispatched two trusty messengers to New Haven to acquaint the governor and assembly.

So that no unfairness could be charged, the two selected were Eli Forest and Remember Baker.

Ethan Allen was seated in his room in the barracks alone smoking a corncob pipe, a favorite with him and most Green Mountain farmers.

A timid knock was heard at the door, and Allen called out cheerily:

"Come in!"

The door opened and Eben entered.

"Why, Eben, you are a stranger; where have you been?"

"In the fort, colonel, almost a prisoner."

"A prisoner?"

"Yes, colonel. That man—pardon me, I mean Col. Arnold—has told me to keep to my own quarters and not move about the fort until I am ordered."

"By what authority?"

"He says he is commander of the fort and will not have me spying round; that is what he calls it."

"I am commander here, and I expect you to obey me."

"Yes, colonel. Did you know that the colonel—Arnold, I mean—is arranging to send ammunition to New Haven?"

"No."

"I heard him give the order."

"You did?"

"Yes, colonel."

"Is Martha Baker still in the fort?"

"Yes, colonel; and I think she would like to stay here until her brother can look after her."

"And you would not object to her staying?"

"No; why should I?"

"I thought that you liked her society."

"So I do, colonel, when I can see her, but Col. Arnold has kept her pretty close in the room which was assigned her."

It was the end of May, and Ethan Allen was waiting news from Boston.

News had just reached him that the Continental Congress, sitting in Philadelphia, had drawn up articles of confederation, and that those articles had been signed by the representatives of thirteen colonies.

And the news also came that on the same day the people of North Carolina had held a convention at Charlotte and declared themselves independent of the British crown, and that they had organized a local government and pledged themselves to raise and equip an army.

This was pleasing news, but Allen wanted to hear more from Boston.

The information conveyed to him by Eben was disquieting.

Was it possible that Benedict Arnold was taking things into his own hands and acting without consulting him?

He sent for Arnold.

"Well, sir, you wished to see me?"

"Yes, colonel; I wanted to know if it were true that you had arranged to send a portion of our cannon and ammunition to New Haven?"

"It is quite true."

"Why did you not consult me?"'

"It was not necessary."

"I am commander here."

"I beg your pardon, Mr. Allen."

Allen passed over the insulting way in which Benedict Arnold addressed him, and very calmly replied:

"You came to me as a volunteer, and I accepted your services and those of your men."

"Quite true."

"Since when, then, have you been given the command?"

"It is time, Mr. Allen, that we should understand each other. I am a commissioned colonel. I bear that rank according to the laws of my colony, Connecticut. Moreover, I was commissioned a colonel by the Provincial Assembly at Cambridge. You hold no rank except that given you by some farmers who have not even the right to elect a representative, but are only squatters on land belonging either to New Hampshire or New York. When the fort was captured it became a military necessity that some one should be in command who would have power to treat with the enemy, and, as you were only—well, a Green Mountain Boy, the command fell upon me."

"Indeed!"

"Yes, and I was thinking of asking you to retire, as your plebeian conduct with the men is apt to injure discipline, and so demoralize the small army."

"You are very considerate."

"It is my duty. I shall take care that your bravery shall be acknowledged."

"Thank you!"

"I must confess that for one who has had no military training you have behaved wonderfully well. The thanks of Connecticut will be awarded to you in due season, and I will see that whatever personal expense you may have been put to shall be reimbursed to you out of the amount voted by the assembly."

"And I suppose you wish the Green Mountain Boys to leave the same time you desire me to go?"

"No, we have need of men. I shall call them all together and ask them to volunteer as soldiers in the new Continental army, and the officers shall retain the rank they hold at present."

"You have developed the plan very fully."

"Yes, and believe me, Mr. Allen, that I only wish that I could ask you to volunteer; you see yourself that it would be impossible."

"Yes, it would."

"Having been the commander, it would be humiliating for you to accept a lower rank, and besides, the men might think you had a right to give general orders, and thus there would be confusion."

"You are right."

"When can you be ready to leave?"

"I do not know."

"What do you say to the first of June?"

"It depends."

"On what? I will give you an escort."

"When I leave I will arrange for my own escort, should I need one. But it was not of that I was thinking."

"Of what, then?"

"The return of the messengers from New Haven."

"That need not bother you. The report will be made to me, as commanding officer."

"Will it?"

"Certainly, so you can arrange to leave on the first of the month."

"Thank you."

"That is settled, then?"

"Is it?"

"Yes. I am very glad, for I have had a very unpleasant task."

Allen had remained so calm that Arnold was deceived.

He staggered like a drunken man when Allen turned on him, and, in tones which could not be misunderstood, said:

"I have heard all you have to say, and I now tell you that in the name of the Great Jehovah I shall remain here as long as I please, or until the general of the Continental Congress removes me, and, what is more, I shall remain in command, and if you dare to interfere with me or my command, by the Great Jehovah I will send you to Philadelphia in irons! You are removed from all responsibility until further orders. Go, or I may forget myself!"

CHAPTER XIX.
NEWS FROM BOSTON.

Benedict Arnold had found his master.

This man, whose ambition was colossal, had imagined that the Green Mountain farmer would quail before him and surrender the command.

Arnold's ambition was plausible. What could a farmer know of military affairs? True, Arnold had been a merchant, but then he had studied at Yale and had made military subjects his special forte, and he had been complimented by soldiers of high repute.

Then, had not the English Capt. Delaplace told him he should be a general, and if he remained with the colonies he should have the command of all the forces the young nation could put into the field?

All this had made him believe himself a great man.

But he had encountered a greater.

Ethan Allen, mountaineer, farmer, amateur soldier, as Arnold had called him, proved to be the superior of the polished Yale graduate.

Arnold retired to his quarters, feeling very glum.

Allen sent for Seth Warner. He wanted some one on whom he could rely.

He told Warner what had happened, and the honest Vermonter suggested that Arnold should be placed under arrest and tried by court-martial.

But such a course Allen would not countenance. He felt that Arnold was not dangerous, and that he could afford to leave him to his own conscience.

"I hear that cannon and ammunition was about to be shipped to New Haven?"

"Yes, colonel; most of the spoil was to be sent there. We all thought that it was by your order."

"Zounds, man! I never heard of it until young Eben told me just now."

"We all thought that he was obeying your instructions, and, therefore, why should we come and tell you?"

"That is so. Do not allow one gun to leave the fort."

Eben entered the room, and was out of breath.

"What is it, Eben?"

"If you please—I—have—news——"

"What is it?"

"I—have been—across—the lake. I——"

"Sit down and get your breath; you will be able to talk plainer. No danger threatens us?"

"No—I—don't think so."

Eben fanned himself and gradually became calmer. But he was so eager to tell his news that he could not wait long enough to be quite coherent.

"News from Boston," he jerked out; and at once Ethan Allen was as much excited as Eben.

"What news? Who brought it? Quick, Eben; don't you see how anxious I am to hear all about it?"

"All the English army has landed at Boston, and they have hanged the men we loved. At least, I think so; I was in so great a hurry that I did not wait to hear all."

"Who brought the news?"

"No one yet. They are riding like the mischief, but I jumped in my boat and paddled across, and then ran like the wind to be first. They are here now."

Two men were admitted into the presence of Ethan Allen and Seth Warner.

After the usual salutes and the presentation of a short letter from Sam Adams, telling Allen that he could believe all the men told him, they were asked to tell their story.

"On the twenty-fifth we saw the great gunboats and the men-of-war in the harbor getting ready for some move. We wondered what they could be doing, but only for a few minutes, for we saw other vessels moving into the harbor, and then the cannon belched forth in salute. The noise deafened us, and the jarring broke lots of windows. We soon knew that ten thousand men had arrived in the harbor, and that England was going to crush us——"

"You mean to try and crush us."

"Yes. Three generals had come over with reinforcements; they were Howe, Clinton and Burgoyne. Gage was like a mad creature. He danced and shouted like a boy getting an unexpected vacation. Then he said he would hang Adams and Hancock with his own hands on Boston Common, but Burgoyne stopped him and suggested trying an offer of pardon——"

"Of pardon?"

"Yes. There is a proclamation signed by Gage, offering pardon to all who will surrender and acknowledge that they have done wrong, except Samuel Adams and John Hancock, and these are said to be guilty of treason and must die; that is, when Gage catches them."

"Well, what say the people?"

"That we will fight it out."

"Good!"

"And that if Adams and Hancock are traitors, so are they all."

"Well?"

"Gage heard of the defiance, and at once gave notice that he should sally out of Boston and burn all the neighboring towns and devastate the country."

"He did, eh?"

"Yes, and the people say they will give him a warm reception."

"Warner, shall we join the men at Boston?"

"You are commissioned to hold Ticonderoga," said the messenger, "and so prevent the British using it against us."

"That we will do. Warner, give orders that all the cannon and the ammunition we can spare be sent as rapidly as possible to the patriots. We must help them all we can."

"That is the right way to talk, colonel; I feel ever so much better now; there is a rope ready for my neck if I fail."

The messengers who brought the news from the patriots of Massachusetts were entertained right royally, and took back with them a good impression of Ethan Allen and his Green Mountain Boys.

But it was not an opinion only that they took back with them, for they had an escort of fifty men, and with them were twenty heavy cannon, with good ammunition, and a promise of as many more heavy guns as soon as horses could be procured to haul them.

"Tell Gen. Gage, if you see him," said Allen, "that the rope which he has for Sam Adams must be long enough and strong enough for Ethan Allen and his Mountain Boys, for they will never surrender as long as they have strength to shoulder a musket or draw a sword."

The day after the men left for Boston a letter from the governor of New Hampshire was received by Allen, ordering him to return home and lay down his sword.

To this letter Allen replied:

"I will gladly lay down my sword, for I hate fighting, but cannot do so until England recognizes the independence of the colonies or until the people themselves have concluded an honorable peace with Great Britain."

Arnold contrived to send a letter to New Hampshire and one to New Haven, in which he reported the "treachery and tyranny of the man Ethan Allen."

There is no proof that either of the recipients did anything save throw the letters into the fire.

On the following day Baker and Forest returned from New Haven, bearing with them the thanks of the colony to Col. Ethan Allen and Col. Benedict Arnold. The latter containing the thanks of the assembly, engrossed on parchment and sealed with the seal of the colony, placed Allen in the first place, and only mentioned Arnold as a coadjutor.

The two emissaries were escorted to Ticonderoga by Col. Hinman and a regiment of Connecticut soldiers.

Hinman was commissioned to aid Allen in any way that he could, and to act under his direction.

Allen, however, determined on a wider field for himself and men than merely remaining as a garrison of a fort, with the mild excitement of an occasional scrimmage with the enemy when out on a foraging expedition, so he handed over the forts to Col. Hinman, taking a receipt for the same.

That curious old document is perhaps the only one in existence of the kind, for it is a receipt for the delivery of the forts of Ticonderoga, Crown Point and Skenesburgh, and is made out much in the same way as a receipt for a few dollars would be.

Arnold was to remain with Hinman for a time, but with the lower rank of major.

With only a small number of followers, including Seth Warner, Remember Baker, Eben Pike and twenty trusty mountaineers, Allen, the hero of Ticonderoga, left the fort and proceeded to Albany.

CHAPTER XX.
A ROADSIDE ADVENTURE.

It was a daring thing to do, but Ethan Allen thought only of his country, and how to benefit the national cause.

The proclamation offering a large reward for him, dead or alive, was still to be seen on the public buildings of the towns and villages through which he passed.

Though every one knew him, for his identity could not be concealed, he was as safe as in his mountain home.

The people of New York were ready to cast in their lot with the colonies which had declared their independence, and, though nominally loyal to England, the Yorkers were only waiting an opportunity to openly throw off the yoke and declare themselves independent.

"The Hero of Ticonderoga," as Allen was called everywhere, was lionized by the people, though those in authority were compelled to appear as though they did not recognize him.

When Allen reached Albany he at once went to the Assembly Hall.

Marching up to the speaker's desk he said, in a loud voice:

"I am Ethan Allen, leader of the Green Mountain Boys, and I have come, not to surrender to you or to lower my claims to the lands in the New Hampshire grants, which we now call Vermont, but to ask you to listen to a plan by which our country may become a nation, free and independent."

"I propose that the assembly go into secret session to hear the Hero of Ticonderoga."

The speaker was one who had been most bitter against Allen when he had appeared there sometime before to argue in favor of the men of Vermont.

"Let it be understood that New York, in listening to Ethan Allen, does not relinquish its claims to the lands which he culls Vermont."

"That matter can well be left in abeyance," said Allen. "There is a greater one—that of our independence as a nation."

"On that subject we will hear you!"

"I ask that the proceedings shall be secret."

"That is understood."

Ethan Allen, with a natural eloquence and rugged fervor, laid before the representatives of the people a plan for the invasion of Canada.

He showed how, with daring and quickness, the country north of the St. Lawrence could be captured, thereby inflicting an injury on the British, and taking from them a large tract of country, which could be made so valuable an adjunct of the colonies south of the St. Lawrence when they became independent.

He had gathered information which showed how easily all Canada could be captured, save, perhaps, the citadel of Quebec.

He was listened to patiently. He was cheered when he spoke of the gallant attack on Quebec by Wolfe and the heroic defense of the French general, Montcalm; and tears rolled down many cheeks when he recalled how the French hero, wounded unto death, expressed a pleasure that he should not live to witness the surrender of Quebec.

Then, with solemn voice, he told how the English had but a small garrison at the citadel, and how it could be taken unawares and maybe captured as easily as Ticonderoga.

In one thing did Ethan Allen fail.

He hinted that perhaps the French Canadians would help the Yorkers and participate in the driving out of the British from North America.

We say that was a mistake, because the people still remember the great struggle against the French, and the fierce war between the colonies acknowledging England and France.

One man, afterward one of the foremost to welcome Lafayette to New York, declared that it would be better to be the slaves of England than the friends of France.

"Better serfdom, degradation, death under England's flag than liberty if obtained by the assistance of France."

His fiery speech turned the tide of feeling against Ethan Allen and the invasion of Canada, and the assembly absolutely refused to listen any further to Allen.

Some were ungenerous enough to taunt him with suggesting the plan on purpose to save himself from arrest.

Others wanted to know if he expected to be the general commanding.

"No, I should have asked permission to join as a private soldier, for I have no ambition to command even a squad."

"What, then, was your object?"

"I live to serve my country; I hope to see her free and independent."

Saying which, he left the hall, and his Mountain Boys were downhearted at the treatment he had received.

"Shall we return to our mountains?" asked Baker.

"No; at least I shall not. I shall journey to Philadelphia and see what the Continental Congress is doing."

"We will go with you."

"I shall be glad of your company, though maybe you have more urgent matters at home to attend to."

"That was unkind, colonel," Seth Warner murmured.

"I meant it not so, believe me. I know that all of you are ready to serve your country."

Albany was left behind and the party started south for Philadelphia.

After a long march a place of rest was sought.

It was nothing unusual for a semi-military company to be on the march, and so the party did not attract any extraordinary attention.

A farmhouse seemed best suited for the refreshment and rest required, and one was found which seemed to answer all purposes.

Warner went forward to interview the farmer, and soon returned with the pleasing news that the party could have supper, rest for the night, and breakfast in the morning for a most moderate sum.

The farmer was hospitable.

He killed some chickens and a young pig, and in a very short time the odor of cooking was very appetizing.

After supper the farmer insisted on bringing out several flagons of good cider, strong and old, for it was the last year's make.

Song and story enlivened the evening.

Warner told of the days when he had hunted the wild bear and met with some startling adventures.

Baker recounted many a stirring episode in the life of a hunter, and Allen, who passed under an assumed name, kept up the interest by narrating a story of ancient knighthood.

"Seems to me that there are as great heroes to-day as in olden times," the farmer remarked.

"Yes, I suppose so."

"Now, in the troubles we are just encountering, there will be opportunities for heroism."

"Yes, and many a brave boy will sleep in a nameless grave."

"That is true; but if we get rid of England's rule and that of the tones, these same boys will rest well in their graves."

"You seem to think the patriots are right."

"I know they are, and I tell you, my masters, that as long as I have a stalk of corn on my farm I'll divide it with any boy who fights against the oppressor."

"Bravo! but methinks the people round about do not think as you do."

"Many are afraid to speak, because, if they did, and the English were successful, they would be made to suffer; and if the patriots win, as I am sure they will, then the silent man may be counted a patriot."

"Very wisely stated."

"My idea of a great man is——"

The farmer paused.

"Excuse me, I thought I heard some one at the window. No, I was wrong, and yet I could have sworn I saw a face as I looked up."

"You were saying that your ideal of a man was——"

"Ethan Allen, the hero of Ticonderoga. I tell you, he is right all the time. He was right about those land grants. If the land had been of no value New Hampshire might have had all the land, but because it proved rich, of course York coveted it."

"Have you ever seen Ethan Allen?" Warner asked.

"No. I would give half my farm to do so."

"You needn't do that. Look at him; that is the hero of Ticonderoga, and I am Seth Warner who tells you so."

The farmer was overjoyed, and became so excited that he shouted and danced with joy.

There was a sudden stop put to his merriment. Something fell over outside the window.

"I could have sworn it before, but now I know some one was there. That milk can could not fall down without hands. I'll find the scurvy wretch and thrash him into sense!"

The milk can had been thrown down, but no one was in sight, and after a search the party returned to the large kitchen, where they again replenished their glasses with cider.

In an interval of the fraternal mirth Eben got close to Allen and asked him to spare a few moments.

"What is it, Eben?"

"I like it not, colonel. Some one was at that window at the time you were discovered, and the knocking over of the milk can was an accident; the man who did it has gone to find some English who will pay well for your capture."

"You are too suspicious, Eben."

"Perhaps so, colonel, but do be careful."

"I will. I have no desire to get into any jail, and I am sure that I like life too well to risk it needlessly."

It was after ten o'clock, a late hour in those days, before the farmer would listen to any suggestion of retiring for the night.

He wanted Allen to sleep in the house—the others were to occupy the hay loft—but Allen declared that he would share the loft with his friends, and that no man should say that he had accepted better treatment than his followers.

As it was impossible for all to stay in the house, the farmer gave way and allowed Allen to share the hay loft.

It was a happy party that climbed up the stairs into the place, where the sweet odor of the hay created a desire for sleep.

In less than ten minutes the hay had been too much for them, and all were asleep.

No, not all, for Eben only pretended to sleep; he was wide awake, for he feared treachery, and determined to be on the alert.

The boy was a natural wonder. He never knew what it was to be tired. He could march farther than most men, eat less and do without sleep, and never did he appear to be the least wearied.

The hour of midnight had passed and the early morning, according to the manner of marking time, had commenced; in other words, it was one o'clock when Eben fancied he heard a slight noise.

He was in a position where he could see everything outside, and as the moon was shining brightly he was not long in discerning a number of men moving toward the barn.

He crawled across to Ethan and gently shook him.

"Colonel, we are betrayed."

Allen was about to jump, when Eben whispered:

"Lie still or you will be seen; the loft door is open. I can wake the others, and would it not be well to let them come right up into the loft before we strike?"

"Eben, you ought to be a general. Wake the others and caution them to lie still."

The boy crawled round the loft and quickly did his work.

When Ethan knew that all were awake he spoke in a loud whisper to them:

"Eben has suggested a plan of campaign and I shall adopt it. We must all pretend to be asleep. Let the English enter the loft, and, when the opportunity arises, let the English be on the ground and the patriots above them."

Every man lay perfectly still, and it really seemed as though Eben had been mistaken, for the time was so long before any attempt was made to enter the loft.

Eben knew all that was transpiring. He saw a man's head rise above the floor and look around, and then he heard the man descend the ladder.

It was fully five minutes after he had reached the ground before he again ascended.

The man crawled along the floor and lay perfectly still.

Another, then another, ascended the ladder, until a dozen soldiers in uniform were in the loft.

Eben was not the only one who had watched their movements, for each of the Mountain Boys had one eye sufficiently open to see them.

A rustling of the hay was the signal given by the sergeant for the English to rise.

Each man rose to his feet and stood over the apparently sleeping colonials.

But no sooner had the enemy taken its position than the mountaineers put out their hands suddenly and grasped the soldiers by the legs.

In an instant every soldier was on his back, thrown to the floor with a violence which he did not relish.

And over each man stood one of the mountaineers, ready to blow out the soldier's brains did he attempt to move.

"Get up!" commanded Allen.

Each man rose, looking very sheepish.

"Hand over your guns and other weapons."

The soldiers obeyed. Not because they desired to do so, but at each man's head was a pistol, and in each pistol was a bullet which meant a nameless grave for the man who received it.

The captured men were made to descend the ladder, but no chance of escape was given them, for at the foot of the ladder stood some of the Mountain Boys, ready to fire if necessary.

There was a coil of rope in the barn, and this Allen utilized in securing the prisoners in a novel fashion. He ordered the men to be tied in couples, the right leg of one to the left leg of his mate, after the fashion of a three-legged race. Then the couples were united by a rope which wound round their arms and passed from one couple to another, to prevent the party separating.

Warner roused the farmer, and that man was so indignant that he proposed shooting each of the prisoners.

"No, no," said Allen, "they only obeyed orders. I shall let them go this time, if they will tell me the name of the informer."

The English soldiers were loyal and refused to purchase their release on such terms.

After an early breakfast Allen was ready to resume his journey, and he ordered the prisoners to march before him.

When the farm had been left behind a distance of a mile, he told the prisoners they were free to go where they liked, but as a precaution against being followed, he did not unfasten them, knowing that it might be hours before they succeeded in getting loose.

CHAPTER XXI.
THE CONTINENTAL CONGRESS.

The old hall in Philadelphia, where the city fathers met, was filled with a notable gathering, representing eleven colonies.

Those men constituted the Second Continental Congress.

The first had been held in October, 1765, and a resolution was adopted declaring that the American colonists, as Englishmen, would not and could not consent to be taxed but by their own representatives. This resolution was called forth through the passage of the "Stamp Act."

The Second Congress assembled in Philadelphia in September, 1774, and pledged the colonies to support Massachusetts in her conflict with the English ministry, and after petitioning the king and the English people, adjourned to meet, as it happened, on the very day that Ethan Allen captured Ticonderoga.

The members of that Congress were all loyal to England. The time for independence had not come.

But what a galaxy of men!

There were such giants among men as Benjamin Franklin, Patrick Henry, Samuel and John Adams, and Thomas Jefferson and George Washington.

But among all those men there was not one whose ambition led him to place self above country.

John Adams told the Congress that the time had come when the English people must learn that it would be better to die fighting for liberty than to live in perpetual slavery.

Not a man wanted war.

Washington had been a soldier with Braddock, and had won distinction, but he was for peace. Jefferson demanded liberty, but he deprecated war. Sam Adams startled the members by saying that if England persisted in a policy of coercion it would be necessary to fight, yet even Adams believed in peace.

John Adams made a strong speech, in which he asked why a tyrant ever exercised tyranny, and he answered the question by saying it was because the people were unable to resist.

"Let us be strong enough to enforce our demands," said he, "and the king or his ministers will fall back and concede all we ask."

He waited to see the effect of his words.

There was silence.

"Yes, brothers, it is only the strong that obtain justice. The weak petition and are spurned, the strong ask and they are listened to with attention, and their demands granted.

"These colonies should be Great Britain's strength, they are her weakness. Give us the right to make our own laws, to raise the taxation as we please, to defend our coasts from external assaults and our land from internal troubles, and we shall honor the king and prove that the American Confederation of Colonies is the strength of that country. Let us tell the king plainly what we want. Let our petition be backed by a good army, and we shall win."

"What do you propose?" asked Jefferson.

"I propose that we organize an army, not of one colony, but of a confederation of all colonies, and that we appoint a commander-in-chief, a man who shall be able to organize the army and to lead it, ay, even if it be necessary until we have entire independence."

"Where could we find such a man?" asked one of the Northern delegates.

"We have one here. The man who saved the wreck of Braddock's army is just the one to build a nation. I nominate George Washington as the commander-in-chief of the army of liberation!"

There was an outburst of cheering such as the Quaker City had but seldom heard.

The delegates knew Washington.

He was a member of the Virginia House of Burgesses, and had previously made a name for himself with Braddock.

When his name was mentioned by Adams he left the hall.

He was afraid to remain for fear he should be called upon to accept.

He wanted time for deliberation.

The congress adjourned until the following Thursday.

The delegates talked the matter over, and when the Congress reassembled George Washington was the unanimous choice of the delegates.

But before he was asked to give his answer, articles of confederation were drawn up and signed, and the colonies became one for the purposes of mutual defense.

"I fear that this day will mark the downfall of my reputation," said Washington to Patrick Henry when he heard he was unanimously selected to organize an army of twenty thousand men, who were undisciplined, without weapons, without arms of any kind worth speaking of, and having no money to pay for the food they would require, not mentioning arms.

The question of salary was next discussed, but Washington stopped it by emphatically declaring that he would not touch one penny of salary, and only asked that out-of-pocket expenses should be paid.

In the midst of the cheering which these words evoked, Ethan Allen entered the hall.

"Who is that man?" asked John Hancock.

"Ethan Allen, the hero of Ticonderoga," answered Sam Adams.

The cheering broke out again, but this time it was for the Green Mountain leader.

Again and again did the walls re-echo with the plaudits.

Then Sam Adams called Ethan Allen to the chairman's desk, and John Hancock warmly congratulated the hero.

A resolution of thanks was passed, and Allen was asked to introduce his friends.

Seth Warner and Remember Baker were welcomed as able coadjutors, and Allen took care to say that they were typical of all the Mountain Boys, and that what they had done was only a foretaste of what they would do if necessary.

Eben Pike was called up, and the boy bashfully wriggled—no one could call it walking—up to John Hancock's desk.

When Allen told of the bravery of the young scout and of the way in which he had so recently saved his friends from falling into the hands of the English, Hancock rose from his seat and called for three hearty cheers for the young hero.

Then the Congress settled down to work and appointed officers to assist Washington.

What a brave lot of men! Their names cannot be too often repeated.

The major-generals were Artemus Ward, Charles Lee, Phillip Schuyler and Israel Putnam—the famous wolf-den Putnam. Then the brigadier-generals comprised Richard Montgomery, Seth Pomeroy, David Wooster, William Heath, Joseph Spencer, John Thomas and Nathaniel Greene. The adjutant-general was Horatio Gates.

Allen overheard Gen. Schuyler speak of Canada and of its importance.

Allen made his acquaintance and asked him to allow him to tell of the plan New York had rejected.

Schuyler was delighted, and thanked the Vermonter warmly.

"If ever you are in command of such an army of invasion," said Allen, "I shall ask to be allowed to join as a volunteer."

"My dear Allen, there is not a man in all Philadelphia at the present moment I would rather have," answered the general.

Alas! what suffering was to follow that conversation!

CHAPTER XXII.
EBEN'S ADVENTURES.

Among the men who were to lead the colonial armies Allen had his attention attracted to Richard Montgomery, who was to share with Schuyler the responsibility of the invasion of Canada.

Montgomery was one of the most fascinating men who rallied to the standard of the colonies.

He was an Irishman, the son of a member of the British parliament, and was educated in Trinity College, Dublin.

In 1754 he obtained a commission in the army, and with his regiment came to this country, and, although only eighteen years old, he distinguished himself for personal bravery in many an action.

In 1760 he was with Gen. Wolfe, and became the adjutant of the regiment.

After distinguishing himself in the expedition against Havana and Martinique, he returned to England and stayed there nine years.

But he yearned for America, and so sold his commission and came to New York, where he married and took a leading part with the sturdy men who refused to bow the knee to English tyranny.

When the Continental Congress was held Montgomery was a delegate, and he pledged his sword in defense of the popular rights.

No wonder that Ethan Allen should be pleased with the Irishman. They were kindred spirits.

Montgomery asked Allen to tell him of the struggle of the Vermonters against the pretensions of New York.

Allen did so, but somewhat bitterly.

"Nay, my dear Allen, do not let that irritate you. We shall soon make common cause, and instead of the colonies we shall have a nation, and we shall be citizens, not subjects."

"Citizens!" Allen repeated.

"Yes, mark me. If the colonies become a nation there will be a free government based on equal rights, and none will be subject to another, but all be equal before the law."

Montgomery saw more clearly into the future than did even Washington.

When the Congress was over, and Washington commenced his work of creating an army, Allen returned home, somewhat disappointed.

He had expected a commission in the new army, but his name was passed over by Congress.

It was afterward proved that the omission was the result of inadvertence, for it was supposed that he had a commission from the general in command of the Colonials at Boston, and the order was made confirming all such commissions.

The summer was passing, and no action had been taken.

Allen was getting weary of the delay.

He could not understand why Boston had not been taken and the English driven out. Then he heard that Benedict Arnold had received a commission, and was leading an army into Canada to attack Quebec.

In despair Allen left his home and crossed to Ticonderoga, determined to offer his services to the Connecticut captain who was in command of the little garrison.

He was sitting on a gun on the day of his arrival on the scene of his great exploit, when a boy, dirty, ragged and half starved, entered the fort and stood opposite Allen.

"Don't you know me, colonel?"

"Is that you, Eben?"

"Yes. I am Eben Pike, and right glad I am to see you."

"How did you enter? Where have you been?"

Eben did not answer. He was too weak. His body swayed, his limbs trembled, and he would have fallen had not Allen caught him.

As gently as a mother carries her child, the hero of Ticonderoga bore the half-famished boy into the barracks and asked that he should receive attention.

The boy was undressed and washed, then little sips of beef tea were given him.

In an hour he showed signs of returning vitality, and they knew that he would live.

"He left here a month ago," explained the captain; "I sent him on a delicate mission, knowing that he could be trusted. When he did not return I thought him dead."

"You knew I should be true to the cause then?" whispered Eben.

"Yes, my boy; no one would ever doubt your loyalty. You shall tell your adventures later. You must rest and get stronger."

"But I have news I must tell. Gen. Montgomery is on his way to Ticonderoga to join Arnold in his invasion of Canada. He will be here to-morrow."

The speech was long for him, and his flushed cheek and quivering voice told how the message had shaken his frame.

Late that night he woke from a good sleep, and seeing Allen by his bed, he put out one hand.

"I am so glad to see you, colonel. I feel all right now. I thought I should die without seeing you."

"Where have you been?"

"I cannot tell you all, but when I left here I fell into the hands of a tory, and he knew me. He called me a spy, and wanted to hang me, but before he could get a rope a new idea came to him. He called some more tories together and they laughed at his suggestion. He wanted to cover me with tar and then set light to it."

"His name? I will serve him that way."

"The tar was poured all over me, and my clothes were saturated with it. But when he went for a light to set me on fire, his little boy, a sweet little fellow, ran from the house and called 'fire,' and just then a flame did break out through the windows. The tory thought more of his house than he did of me, so I ran away as fast as I could."

Eben rested after telling that adventure, and it was more than an hour before he could resume his narrative.

"I ran as fast as I ever did in my life, and, as bad luck would have it, I fell into the hands of some English soldiers. They did not know me, and thought I was some ignorant country lad, so I fared pretty well, and only stayed with them two days. When they broke camp they insisted that I should go with them, and as I had told them I was going in the very direction they intended going, I could not help myself."

"You were in hard luck."

"Yes, but that was not the last of my adventures, for I was recognized by another tory, who had been birched by some of our men for his treachery. He claimed me as his prisoner, and to get me had to swear that I was his apprentice, who had run away."

"And of course the soldiers gave you to him?"

"Yes, and a nice time I had of it. The farmer stripped me and then gave me fifty strokes with a strong cane — —"

"The villain!"

"But that was not the worst. He threw me naked into a cellar and kept me without food until I began to lose my senses, and then he gave me these old clothes and some food. I managed after a long time to escape, and for a week I wandered about the woods, living on what I could pick up, until I managed to reach here. I dare not go to a house, for the tories were searching for me, and I was afraid to even jump into the river for fear that I might be seen and have no chance of escape."

"Poor fellow. So you failed in obtaining the information for which you set out."

"Failed? No, I got it, and though it is a trifle late, I find it is in time."

Col. Hinman was so pleased with the thoroughness of Eben in everything he undertook that he sent a special dispatch to Gen. Washington, commending Pike as one of the best scouts and secret service officers any country could produce.

Hinman tried to persuade Ethan Allen to join him, but the Green Mountain hero wanted more stirring work than could be found in a fort which might never be attacked.

The news that Montgomery was near the fort was sweetest music to him, and he resolved to unite with his army, even as a private soldier.

CHAPTER XXIII.
FORAGING.

Eben's news was in every point correct. Gen. Schuyler had been stricken down by sickness, and Montgomery assumed command of one of the armies of invasion.

Allen went out to meet the Irish general and received a warm welcome.

Montgomery was full of praise of the plan of invasion.

Arnold and Morgan were marching through Maine to attack the citadel of Quebec, and Montgomery was to march into Canada to the westward, and after capturing Montreal and other important places, form a junction with Arnold and drive the English out of Quebec.

"That man has a great brain," Montgomery remarked, as he told Allen the plan.

"To whom do you refer?"

"Gen. Benedict Arnold."

"What has he done?"

"He formulated the plan and sent it to Gen. Washington——"

"He did?"

"Yes, and the commander was so pleased with it that he wrote a personal letter to Arnold, thanking him and saying that the plan should be put into immediate execution."

"And Arnold really took the credit, if credit there be?"

"Of course; why not?"

"I am not surprised, and yet— —"

"You are not jealous?"

"Jealous? No, not of a thief."

"A thief?"

"Yes, a thief. I drew up that plan and copied it in duplicate, so that if one got lost the other would remain. I took one copy to Albany and laid it before the assembly."

"And the copy?"

"I left it at Ticonderoga."

"What became of it?"

"I do not know; at least I find that I know now, though I had no suspicion. When I returned from the Continental Congress I asked for the plan, and was told it had been lost. The truth is that Arnold took it away with him."

"Gen. Washington shall know this."

"No, never mind. I care not who gets credit for the plan if it is only successful; but if I should fall let the people of Vermont know that the plan was mine."

"Rest assured of that."

"I have the original with me, and you shall read it, for I want no one to accept my word for anything."

Allen was right. Benedict Arnold had read the plan, and had actually appropriated the copy and sent it in Allen's writing to Philadelphia.

Once he was asked about Allen's statement, and he replied that he had employed Ethan Allen to make copies from his rough draft.

The young Irish general of division did not believe in loitering, and after a day's rest at Ticonderoga the march was resumed.

Allen had joined, but having no commission, he was placed in rather a delicate position, though the very fact that he was, in a sense, a freelance, made him more valuable to Montgomery.

A promise was given that, should an opportunity offer, Allen was to command a regiment under Montgomery.

After leaving Ticonderoga the march was easy for two days, for the country was peopled by friends of the colonial cause; but after that the farmers were decidedly hostile.

There was great difficulty in feeding the army, and although the general offered to purchase food, the tories refused to sell any.

Allen was commissioned to take twenty men and forage.

He knew that the farmers were tories, but he shrank not from his task.

He was supplied with a small amount of money, and was empowered to pay, by notes, for any food he secured.

About a mile from camp a poultry farm was reached, and Allen at once requisited all the poultry.

The farmer demurred, but the soldiers were the strongest, and very soon a quantity of young turkeys, hens and ducks were in the wagons, much to the delight of the foragers.

At the next house a determined opposition was organized.

At the fence the patriots were met by a number of men, armed with all sorts of weapons.

"We are prepared to pay for what we get," said Allen.

"I guess you will pay for what you get; that would be right easy, for you'll not get a durn thing."

"My friend, you make a mistake."

"Move on there or I'll set the dogs on you."

To emphasize his assertion he whistled, and immediately two splendid animals sprang to his side.

"Call off those dogs; we do not war on dumb animals," Allen called.

"I guess I'll not call 'em off. At' em, beauties."

The dogs sprang over the fence, and with glaring eyes and open mouths made for the nearest soldier.

Two pistol shots prevented them doing any damage, and Allen gave the order to his men to charge the obstructives and take whatever food they could find.

However determined men may be, they cannot stand against muskets and swords, when their weapons are only hay forks and crowbars.

The farm helpers were driven back, and a wagon was quickly loaded with flour and grain and vegetables.

The foraging expedition was a great success, though Allen would have preferred purchasing the food, if any could have been found to sell.

The next day he was sent out again, and met with good success until he was ready to return.

A company of soldiers had been quartered on one of the farms by the English, and Allen was unprepared for the encounter.

When he found he was in for a fight, he felt better satisfied to think he met foemen worthy of his steel, instead of a set of half-fed and badly armed farmers' men.

The English can fight well, and Allen knew that his troops were inferior in every way to the enemy, but he did not hesitate.

"Men, we are outnumbered, but we are not beaten; shall we retire as prisoners, or fight until death claims us?"

"Fight!"

"We cannot surrender without a struggle."

"Who can tell but we may defeat them?"

Allen, pleased with the speeches of his comrades, gave the order to charge the enemy.

The fight was a sharp one.

Hand-to-hand struggles always partake more of the brutish, and the truth about such encounters is far more horrible than any description.

Allen was in the thickest of the fight all the time; his sword was dripping with blood every time he raised it above his head, and that was just as frequently as he could free his arm from the crush to wield his weapon.

Only a few minutes did the struggle last, but the carnage was out of all proportion to the number engaged.

Seven of Allen's men were killed, while the enemy lost twelve, and what seemed remarkable, all who fell were dead. No one seemed to be wounded or maimed; death came to all who were stricken.

The return journey was a sad one, though from the point of view of a soldier it was glorious.

Montgomery congratulated the mountaineer on his bravery, and told him that his record should be known at headquarters.

The next day the march was resumed, and through lack of guides the army took a wrong course.

The vanguard, in crossing a wide stretch of what seemed level country, found themselves in a marsh, and up to their waists in water.

The worst of it was that the bottom was treacherous, for the soil seemed like quicksand, and drew them in until they had difficulty in raising their feet.

After considerable floundering about they got out of the marsh just in time to warn the main body of the army.

The adventure was amusing except to the participants, and many a laugh was had at the expense of the unlucky men.

After a number of strange adventures the army reached Isle-aux-Noix, where Montgomery intended to camp for a time.

Two days after reaching there Allen was delighted to welcome Eben Pike, who had promised to follow as soon as his strength was regained.

He looked as hearty as ever, though less effeminate than when he first joined the Green Mountain Boys.

He had a man's strength, though his appearance was deceiving.

He had such an excellent idea of topography that Allen knew he would be extremely useful to the army of invasion.

CHAPTER XXIV.
SECRET SERVICE.

Gen. Montgomery summoned Allen to his presence one morning early.

"Ethan Allen, you are the one man wanted in this crisis."

"What crisis? What can I do?" asked Allen, looking somewhat surprised at the general's earnestness.

"We are about to invade Canada, and the people ought not to be hostile."

"I fancy you will find them to be so."

"That's just where you will be of value?"

"I do not understand."

"I want you to go into Canada and tell the people that we are not going to fight against them, their country or religion, but only against the English garrisons."

"And I suppose you mean enlist the French on our side?"

"If you can do so, yes."

"When am I to start?"

"As early as possible. Take some good interpreters with you, for French and Indians must be reached and converted."

"The less number of men the better."

"I agree with you, though you know the consequence if you fall into the hands of the enemy."

"Yes, life would be short; but if I can serve my country I will dare anything."

"Spoken like a brave man."

"I am ready. I will take Eben Pike with me, and Remember Baker."

"But you will want an interpreter."

"Yes, one who can talk with the Indians as well as the French."

"You do not mean to enlist the Indians?"

"Yes; I will attract to our side every man, and I would every animal, if that were possible."

"What do you think of Old Buckskin?"

"Do you know him?"

"Yes, and he is with us."

"Just the man. Old Buckskin knows every inch of the ground from here to Quebec. I am glad he is ready to go with me."

The man called Old Buckskin was an eccentric trapper. No one knew his real name, and it is within the realm of probability that he had forgotten it himself.

Allen had met him frequently in the Green Mountains, and knew that he was an excellent guide, a fearless man and a good hunter.

The next day the little party started from St. Valentin and worked northward in the direction of St. John.

The people of Pte. la Mull received Allen with great acclaim, for they were French and had suffered much from the constant interference of the English with their customs and the exercise of their religion.

But they warned him against the people of Sabrevous, for they were so much opposed to the New Yorkers that they could not believe anyone who hailed from that colony, or any colony south of the St. Lawrence, could be friendly to them.

That was enough for Ethan Allen.

His mission was not to convert those who were friendly, but to gather in those who were ranked among his enemies.

Turning eastward, he started for Sabrevous, and with greater enthusiasm than he had felt up to that time.

Allen and his party were dressed ostensibly as merchants, and he professed to be in search of rare skins, to fill an order.

To give color to this assertion, Old Buckskin had brought with him a skin of the rarest color and kind, and Allen declared he should never rest until he had matched it.

No one knew better than Allen, unless it was Old Buckskin, that it would be the most difficult thing to find that shade of natural wool, and so the ruse was successful.

Early one morning, for the march was slow, a man approached the party and stopped Allen.

In French he asked if he was the merchant in search of a peculiar skin.

Allen answered in the affirmative.

"I can take you to the place where you can get as many as you want."

"I will reward you."

"Follow me."

"Where to?"

"Follow me and you shall have the skins at your own price."

"Remember that you have said at my own price."

"Yes; my friends are poor and they will sell cheaply, for food to a starving person is better than the most costly skins."

Old Buckskin whispered:

"Be on your guard."

Allen nodded.

Remember Baker was bolder and asked the French Canadian how he knew they wanted skins.

The man laughed, and answered with an appearance of genuine truth:

"I was at La Mull and heard the monsieur ask about skins."

"Then why did you not speak?"

"I had to see if my friends would sell."

"And you saw the sample?"

"I saw the skin that trapper carried."

That seemed satisfactory, and Allen was quite prepared to follow the Canadian.

Eben was the next to express a doubt. He drew Allen on one side.

"I have seen him somewhere before; do not trust him."

"Imagination, my dear Eben, pure imagination. The man is a French Canadian."

The man had stood on one side, apparently taking no notice of the whispered conversation, but a close observer would have seen that he was watching through the corner of his eye every movement, and if he could read the lips, as so many of his countrymen could, he doubtless knew what was being said.

"Will the monsieur come and see the skins?" he asked.

"Yes; lead on."

The man led the way and Allen and his little band followed.

Many times the guide turned round to see if all were following.

A dense wood lay right before them, and the prospect did not seem very inviting, though no danger could come to them, seeing that they were six in all, and the Frenchman was alone.

"Where are you taking us?" Allen asked.

"To where the skins are."

"How far is it?"

"Not far; if my friends did not want the money very badly I should not bother so much."

As he spoke he fell back so that he was beside Ethan Allen.

"You come from York?" he asked.

"Yes."

"Ah, monsieur, it is a pity that the Yorkers like us not."

"But they do like you."

"You may; your heart is large, and you would buy from a poor Canadian; most Yorkers would steal the skins and kill the Canadian."

"You are wrong. The Yorkers are very anxious to be friends with the people of Canada."

"They hate the Anglais?"

"No, they do not hate the English, though they would like to see the English leave the country, so that the Canadians and the Americans could govern themselves."

"Do you think there will be war?"

"Perhaps."

"Monsieur knows there will be."

"I do not know. I hope not. War would interfere with business."

The Canadian laughed heartily, as though Allen had perpetrated a good joke.

Then he broke into a French song, full of life and character, such as the French peasantry love to indulge in.

Eben took advantage of the song to walk beside Alien and whisper to him his doubts.

"That man is not a Canadian, or if he is, he is an English Canadian."

"What makes you think so?"

"His accent."

"But, Eben, he speaks French fluently."

"Yes, like a Frenchman, not a Canadian."

"What do you know about it?"

"In my young days"—Allen had to smile at the boy referring to his young days—"in my young days I used to know a French boy and a Canadian Frenchman, and they could scarcely understand one another. The French boy used to say, 'You talk French, bah, bah!' and the Canadian used to ask the other why he did not speak proper French."

"I had no idea that you were a linguist."

"If you mean by that that I can talk languages, you are wrong, for I cannot, but I am sure that our guide is not a French Canadian."

"You are too suspicious, and I really do not see what difference it makes what he is; we shall get to know the country and——"

"Miss our way back."

"You think that it is all a trap?"

"I do."

"You will see that you are wrong."

"I hope so, but I am going forward a little."

Eben did not wait for permission, but ran ahead of the party like a wild boy out for a holiday.

The Canadian called him back, but Eben professed not to hear.

In a few minutes he was seen running back toward them.

"Where have you been, Eben?"

"In the forest."

In a lower voice he said:

"There are three houses just ahead, and I am sure I saw a redcoat at one of the doors."

Did the Canadian hear him, or did he judge by intuition?

"Did you see the houses?" he asked Eben, and the question was translated.

"Yes, and I saw a man with a red coat."

"That is good; my brother has got home. He always wears a red shirt. I am so glad."

And to prove his joy he began singing loudly, and through the trees came back the echo of the refrain.

"That is Jacques; I should know his voice wherever I heard it," said the Canadian, resuming his singing as soon as he had uttered the words.

"Please turn back," pleaded Eben.

"You silly fellow, what harm can we come to?"

Although Allen spoke lightly he whispered to his followers to have their pistols ready in case of a surprise.

All saw the houses, poor, miserable dwellings they were, too, but such as were often met with in the woods of Canada.

"Here we are!" cried out the Canadian, "and monsieur shall soon see the skins. Will he pay a good price for them?"

"Yes, if they are what I require."

"They will be."

There was no sign of life at the house, though the guide called:

"Jacques—Jacques!"

"Where can he have got to? Enter, monsieur, and I will find the man who has the skins."

Allen, followed by the others, entered the house, which seemed to consist of one room and an extension kitchen downstairs, and a room upstairs.

In a few minutes a man dressed in a red shirt entered, and said his brother had sent him to entertain them, as he would be detained getting some skins he believed the messieurs wanted.

Everything seemed so quiet and innocent that even Eben was inclined to think he had been unjustly suspicious.

But while Jacques chattered—and he did so rattle along that it was quite impossible for anyone to get in a word—there was a movement outside which was ominous had Allen but known it.

Jacques was telling a hunting story and raised his voice at a most exciting point, when the door was quickly opened and a dozen soldiers from the neighboring garrison sprang into the room and demanded the surrender of the party.

It was impossible to decline the unpleasant invitation, for at each head was a pistol.

As Allen raised his head and looked at the door, he saw the pseudo guide, grinning like a hyena, and in a voice which was very English the man emphasized his laugh by saying:

"Ha, ha, ha! trapped! I have followed Ethan Allen all the way from Ticonderoga, and waited until I could be sure he would be hanged. Now I denounce him as a spy!"

CHAPTER XXV.
DIPLOMACY.

"You denounce me?"

"Yes, I say that you are Ethan Allen, the man who surprised the garrison at Ticonderoga."

"Am I to understand that these soldiers have listened to the ravings of a creature like you?"

The sergeant in command of the squad saluted Allen, and replied:

"I am compelled to obey orders. This man reported that he could lead into ambush one Ethan Allen, and I was detailed to effect his arrest."

"Sergeant, I acknowledge that you have a duty to perform, but cannot a merchant pass through Canada without being suspected of being a spy?"

"With that I have nothing to do; I must ask you to surrender."

"The asking is compulsion. With a pistol at each head, how can we do anything else but surrender?"

Allen wished to delay surrender as long as possible, for he was a firm believer in the doctrines of possibility, and a chance of escape might present itself.

The sergeant laughed at Allen's question.

"It does look like surrender or death, but my orders were to take Ethan Allen, dead or alive."

"Is he then so much feared?"

"If you are Ethan Allen it may be some consolation to know that he is hated by the British authorities more than any man who has joined the American rebels; and if you are not Ethan Allen, as I hope you are not, then you may know that it is a great honor to be mistaken for such a rebel."

"Logical, very. We are merchants in search of skins of a very peculiar shade of color. We work for a customer who is willing to pay largely for such skins—dyed ones will not do—and this fellow pretended that he was French, could not speak English, and told my trapper that he knew where we could get the skins. In all trust we followed. Now I ask you: Is it likely that this Ethan Allen would allow himself to be entrapped?"

"No, you are right; but I am not the judge, and you will have to go to Sabrevous and see the colonel."

"That will take time, and I am anxious to get the skins. I will make you a proposition: I will go with you to Sabrevous, but this man must go with me, and as a prisoner, for I have charges to make against him which will cause him to be hanged. My friends must go free to search for the skins."

"I cannot accept the offer—all must go."

"But you said you were to arrest Ethan Allen; now, we cannot all be Ethan Allen, and I am the one accused."

Allen knew just as well as the officer that all must surrender, but he wanted to confuse the Englishman, and perhaps find a way of escape.

"I am very sorry, but if you are Allen, the party with you may be also wanted. I must demand the surrender of all."

"Before I surrender I demand the arrest of that man."

"What for?"

"Murder!"

The informer almost shrieked as he heard the charge. His knees trembled, the blood left his cheeks, and he looked a most guilty wretch.

"Look at him," Allen exclaimed. "Tell me, is he not guilty?"

"I did not do it. He—he shot himself."

"And you took the skins. Ah, my fine friend, Frenchman or Canadian, you may well tremble. England does not accept the services of murderers. You sought to save yourself by denouncing me. Your trick has failed. I shall not surrender on the accusation of a murderer. I will give my parole to appear against you on your trial."

"You refuse to surrender?" asked the sergeant, in amazement.

"If my accuser was a man of honor instead of a murderer I should bow to fate, but unless you have some one to accuse me who is not tainted I shall resist you, and if I fall my family will hold you accountable for my death."

The sergeant was in a quandary.

He had been ordered to arrest Ethan Allen, and here was a man who had put him to the proof. The only accuser was one whose word was of no account, for he was a self-confessed murderer.

"Are you Ethan Allen?" the sergeant asked, most innocently.

"If you think so arrest me. I shall not answer any questions except before a proper tribunal."

"You are a brave fellow, and I wish there was some one here who knew you."

"I know him!"

All turned toward the door and saw a man with a long white beard and patriarchal appearance, though his garb was that of a monk.

"I know him," the monk repeated. "And I say that, whatever his name may be, he is an honest man."

"You said you knew him, and yet do not know his name; is not that strange?"

"Not at all. In these troublous days a man may have more names than there are days in the week, and yet be honest."

"By what name did you know him?" asked the officer.

"As one who did good wherever he might be."

"He is accused — —"

"The man who accuses him of wrongdoing must be bad at heart, for I will swear that he is innocent."

"But they say he is a spy?"

"A spy? Accuse him of being a spy? Why, one might as well accuse me. He is too open for a spy, and if he was one he would acknowledge it."

"And so criminate himself?"

"If he were a spy, I repeat, he would never deny it if put to the test. Who is his accuser?"

"This man — —"

"That shivering wretch! He looks half dead."

"He will be dead soon," Allen interjected, "for he is a murderer, as well as one who bears false witness against his fellows."

"You say that you believe that miserable reptile, instead of this honest man? Beside, think of the illogical position. If this man is a spy, you have to admit that there is a war between your people and his, and that your government denies."

"I am a soldier and must obey orders."

Allen rose in the dignity of his manhood, and rather startled his own friends by saying:

"I never asked a man yet to disobey orders. Do your duty. I will go with you to Sabrevous; but, mark me, I shall hold your government responsible for my loss of time and for the indignity of this arrest."

Eben Pike had not been under arrest, and now he stood at the door, waiting developments. He saw clearly what should be done. If Allen was condemned, then Montgomery must be informed, and a quick move made on Sabrevous and Allen liberated.

The procession was formed and Eben walked at a little distance from the party, apparently taking no more interest in the affair than one of idle curiosity.

The accuser was pinioned, a musket being secured under his arms across his back, but Allen and his friends were allowed to march entirely unfettered.

The monk, whom we have recognized as the "mad monk" who rescued Martha Baker, walked by the side of the sergeant, while Remember Baker walked with Allen, the soldiers marching in front and rear of the small party.

"How did you know that he was a murderer?" Baker whispered, pointing to the miserable informer.

"I cannot tell. I felt that he was. I had but one thing to guide me. A trapper was found murdered near Ticonderoga, and I heard that the one last seen with him was a fellow who could talk French as well as

English, and I guessed this man might be the one, so I hazarded the accusation, and struck the bull's-eye."

"What will become of us?"

"Cannot say; but Eben is on the alert, and unless they shoot us without the usual twenty-four hours' reprieve, he will have Montgomery come to our rescue."

"Did you give him instructions?"

"Only general ones; he is wide awake, and knows just as well as I do what ought to be done."

"Don't you think the 'mad monk' will betray us?"

"No; he is a sympathizer with our cause, and — — Let us change the subject; one of these soldiers is getting suspicious."

When the party reached Sabrevous the sergeant handed his prisoners over to the proper authorities and reported that he was convinced that a mistake had been made, and that the prisoners were peaceful merchants and not American rebel spies.

The monk was examined in secret, and he also bore testimony to the truth and honor of the chief prisoner.

The accuser was called and asked about the murder he had committed, and under the terror of the accusation he made a full confession, but asked for mercy, because he had followed Ethan Allen and handed him over to the authorities.

His plea for mercy helped Allen, for the English officer believed that the accusation against Allen was only made to obtain favor with the authorities.

He was remanded to prison until the civil power could take him and mete out the punishment he merited.

Allen and his party received the apologies of the officers for their arrest and detention, and were at once liberated.

It had been a narrow escape, but they did not value their liberty any the less for that fact.

Some weeks afterward Allen learned that the officers had been severely reprimanded for allowing the "rebel spy" to escape.

CHAPTER XXVI.
AN INTERESTING EXPERIMENT.

Two days later Allen was not so fortunate.

He had been talking to the people and urging them to remain neutral, allowing the soldiers on each side to fight out the issue, when one of the people of the little town, near which was a small fort, left the house and ran to the fort.

"Ethan Allen, the rebel, is at my house," he cried, almost breathlessly, as he reached the outworks. Instantly there was commotion among the garrison. It was true Allen was dreaded by the British more than the men who were besieging Boston.

He was a freelance, and it was never known where he might strike.

His daring at Ticonderoga was not forgotten, and although no money reward was offered for his arrest, it was known that promotion would be the reward of those who captured him.

A small force was sent at once to the farmhouse and Allen called on to surrender.

The lieutenant who had been consigned to the lead was of a different nature to the sergeant of Sabrevous, for he would not listen to any speech.

"I am here to arrest you and your party, and save your breath, for you will need it at the court-martial. Surrender or we shall make you."

"We shall not surrender," answered Allen, calmly.

Allen, Baker and Old Buckskin had got into a corner of the room and dragged tables and a heavy dresser in front of them.

The English fired at the "rebels" and succeeded only in damaging the walls and furniture.

Old Buckskin raised his musket, an old friend that had brought down many a bear and wolf in the forests; he patted it affectionately and took aim.

Every movement was as calm as though the enemy was a defenseless animal destined to fall beneath the unerring aim of the hunter.

The soldiers had reloaded and awaited the order to fire.

The musket belched forth its leaden fury, and the lieutenant fell dead.

"No use tackling small fry when the big uns are there," explained the hunter, as he reloaded.

Allen and Baker had both fired their pistols and wounded two of the soldiers.

"Let us charge them," suggested Allen, and almost before the words were uttered the little band of patriots had emerged from behind their barricade and were pressing the English toward the door.

With their leader dead, and four more dead or wounded, the soldiers became demoralized, and throwing away their guns, ran just as fast as they would had a pack of hungry wolves been in pursuit.

"Shall we pursue?" asked Baker.

"No, we will return to the camp. I think we have done all we can this trip."

The return to the Isle-aux-Noix was accomplished without any adventure, and Allen was warmly welcomed by Gen. Montgomery.

The young Irish leader had just determined on the siege of St. John, and the information that Allen could give him proved very useful.

The whole plan of campaign was discussed and considerably modified after Allen had given his views on the subject.

The Green Mountain warrior suggested that the besiegers should be protected by what is termed circumvallation—that is, by a line or series of works surrounding the place, not to serve offensively against the place, but to defend the siege army from an attack from without.

His plan was adopted and the work was intrusted to him.

The English in St. John watched the preparations and laughed at the absurdity of the affair.

"Those rebels think they can fight," said the colonel in command. "Let them make all their preparations, and we will blow them all into smithereens in no time."

But as he watched the works proceed he was not quite so sanguine.

"Who is leading the rebels?" he asked.

"Gen. Richard Montgomery."

"Montgomery? Not the Irish general who was with the British at Martinique?"

"The same, Colonel."

"By Jove! by Jupiter! he knows what he is doing. Who is second in command?"

"Ethan Allen."

"By Jove! we have blundered. We ought never to have allowed them to come so near. I thought that they were an undisciplined lot of peasants, who knew nothing about war, and would flee as soon as we opened fire on them."

"Perhaps the rank and file will."

"They dare not."

"Why?"

"I was with Montgomery at Havana, and I know that he would turn his gun on his own men if they showed any signs of retreating. He is the very devil when fighting."

"What shall we do?'

"I must think."

The colonel had shown his anxiety more than he had intended, and he must have some time to recover his equilibrium.

In a few minutes he had taken his glass and scanned the enemy's works.

He saw the weak spots and gave orders that they should be charged.

A regiment sallied out and marched with band playing and banners flying.

Allen saw them approach, and at once communicated with Montgomery.

Orders were given to defend the weak places and to be content in holding the line.

The British had underestimated the courage of the Americans.

They had yet to learn that men fighting for a principle were stronger than those who fought to obey orders.

Allen knew that many of his men were raw, never having stood up before an enemy, and that when it came to fighting they might be frightened.

He called his officers together and addressed them.

"It is necessary that we reduce St. Johns, and as it is our first real battle you must each be responsible for your men. Don't let any falter. At the first sign of retreat, unless I order it, shoot the leader; that will prevent the others from running. It is harsh, but necessary. Now remember that our country depends on us for victory. We must prove ourselves worthy. Address your companies and inspire them with courage. Let each man do his duty."

There was a magnetism about Allen which won respect and obedience.

"Do you not think he blundered?" an officer once asked another about the great Napoleon.

"Blundered? Perhaps he did. But if he ordered me to cut off my hand I would do it. He owns me body and soul."

And it was just this kind of feeling which animated the men who followed Ethan Allen.

The British regiment charged the earthworks, and the Americans had all they could do to hold their position.

The slaughter was large in proportion to the number engaged, and Allen feared for the result.

But when the English began to retire he ordered his men to follow and challenge to another combat.

The enemy, seeing the move, turned and prepared to resist the charge of the Americans.

Then commenced a series of masterly feints which won renown for the Green Mountain hero.

His men fell back after the first volley, and the English pursued.

Again Allen rallied his men and charged the enemy, only to retreat as quickly as before.

Three times was this maneuver practiced, and each time the English were drawn nearer the strongest points of the line of circumvallation.

Montgomery saw, at first with surprise, the movements of his able coadjutor; then, when the object became apparent, he ordered his division to be in readiness, and after the third feint, with a loud shout the entire force of the Americans charged the English and pursued them into the town, slaughtering them like sheep.

Allen advised forcing an entrance into the town, but Montgomery knew that the enemy would have every advantage, and that success was very doubtful.

He preferred to wait, and by strengthening his position compel the garrison to surrender.

The afternoon saw the white flag floating over both fort and earthworks. The emblem of peace meant that both sides wished to care for the wounded and bury the dead.

It is a strange feature of civil war, and the war between the English and the Americans might be so called, that when the flag of truce is hoisted the men of both sides are ready to fraternize.

It was so in this instance before St. Johns.

Men who had been aiming at each other an hour previously now drank from the same canteen and helped to bury each other's dead.

Among the wounded was young Eben Pike.

He was not a soldier; that is, he had never been enrolled among the men, but, as it was afterward known, he had borrowed the uniform of a sick soldier and had answered the name when it was called.

Remember Baker was in command of the burying party, and when he saw Eben he could not help the tears falling on the white face of the boy.

"My poor fellow, are you badly hurt?" he asked, in a tremulous voice.

"I think I have received my call," answered Eben, bravely.

"I hope not. But is there anything I can do for you?"

"I would like to see the colonel."

Eben was placed on a stretcher and carried to the rear.

Very soon Allen was bending over him and asking him about his wounds.

"I do not know; I don't seem to bleed much, and yet I am so weak."

The surgeon came quickly at the request of Allen, and made a thorough examination of the boy.

He was very silent, and no one knew what his verdict would be.

"Am I going home?" asked Eben.

"Going home? Are you tired of fighting?" the surgeon queried.

"Oh, no, I would like to live and fight until my country is free."

The speech was too much for Eben, for he fainted, and the doctor, after leaving instructions, went out of the shed which served as hospital, and called Allen on one side.

"Well?"

"That boy is shocked. It is a peculiar case. Not once in a score of years do we find such a case. Every nerve is numb, every muscle relaxed, and whether he will live or die depends on arousing him from that numbness."

"Is he wounded?"

"Only slightly. A spent ball may have caused the shock. What can we do to rouse him?"

"That is for you to suggest. What do you think necessary?"

"A counter shock of some kind. Its effects would soon be apparent. If it succeeds he will be all right in a day; if it fails he will die."

"And without the counter shock?"

"His life is in a very precarious condition."

"I do not know—how would it be to make believe I am killed?"

"The very thing. I will arrange it."

The doctor laid his plans for the very interesting experiment with great care.

After giving instructions he returned to Eben's cot and felt his pulse. It was very feeble, and life was fast ebbing away. That was the best moment to shock him, and on the effect of that shock his life would depend.

The doctor gave the signal he had arranged, and almost instantly a pistol shot was heard.

Then a second followed.

Eben opened his eyes and looked round.

A cry pierced the walls of the miserable temporary hospital.

"Ethan Allen killed! Who could be his murderer?"

The words were shouted out as though some one was in great distress over the great tragedy.

"What did he say?" asked Eben.

"It sounded like 'Ethan Allen murdered,' but, perhaps, I am mistaken."

"Go and see. Stay, I will go, and if any one has killed the best man on earth I will find him and kill him!"

The blood was coursing faster through the boy's veins; the color had come back to his cheeks and he forgot his wound. His only thought was about Allen.

"You stay here; I will go and see about it."

"Let me go, please do, doctor?"

"No, you stay here. If the report is true you will need all your strength to avenge the death of the brave man."

"You are right. But, doctor, I feel right enough. I wonder what made me think I was going to die?"

"I will tell you all later. Now lie still. I will not be gone long."

"Don't be a minute, please, doctor, or I shall have to come after you."

The surgeon smiled to himself with great satisfaction as he sought the presence of Ethan Allen.

"Well, how did it go?" asked the mountaineer.

"Like magic. No sooner did he hear the cry than he wanted to get up and seek your murderer. He is as well as ever he was, though he will be weak for a day or so."

"Shall I go and see him?"

"Not yet. Wait until I summon you."

The doctor returned to Eben.

"Well, doctor, it is not true—say it is not true!"

"No, the alarm was a false one."

"Thank Heaven!"

"I am just as well pleased as you. Now try and get some sleep."

"Will you ask the colonel to call and see me?"

"Yes. Ah, here he is."

Eben caught Allen's hand and the hot tears flowed over it. He kissed the hard hand of the mountaineer and stroked it until nature came to the rescue and Eben fell back asleep.

"He is saved. The countershock did what nothing else could. It was an interesting experiment."

CHAPTER XXVII.
A PRISONER.

Three days later Allen received another command to penetrate into Canada and seek to interest the Canadians, especially the French, in the colonial cause.

The Green Mountain Boy would have preferred to stay with the army and participate in the siege of St. John, but he was a soldier, and a soldier's first duty is obedience.

He addressed the people in every town and village, and the result was far beyond his expectations.

In a week he had traversed the country as far as St. Ours, twelve miles south of Sorel, and had enlisted two hundred and fifty Canadians and had armed them.

He wrote to Montgomery, telling him of his success, and adding that he hoped to be with him in three days to take part in the assault on St. John.

The return march was commenced, and on the second day the advance guard encountered a regiment of Americans under command of Maj. Brown.

Allen was delighted to meet a brother officer, and regretted that he had sent half his men forward under command of Remember Baker.

Brown was sanguine and saw a chance of striking a great blow at the English power.

"Montreal," he said, "is defenseless, and, with your forces united to mine, we can capture it."

Allen fell in with the suggestion, and a plan was discussed.

The men had met on the east bank of the St. Lawrence, between Longueuil and Laprairie, and it was arranged that Allen was to cross the river in canoes a little north of the city, while Brown and the men under his command were to cross to the south, and, advancing from different directions, make themselves masters of the works and the garrison.

The difficulty of obtaining canoes delayed Allen.

He sent up and down the river to get boats, either by purchase or by force, but only succeeded in getting a very few.

He had to cross and recross three times before he landed his little party on the opposite side.

The night was squally. The wind blew in fearful gusts, and often the frail boats were in danger of being wrecked.

Allen cheered his men and promised them a glorious victory.

It was sunrise before all had crossed, and then the little party awaited the signal from Maj. Brown.

An hour passed and no signal was heard.

Half an hour more, and then Allen knew that Brown had not crossed.

His position was critical.

He would have retreated had it been possible, but he would be seen by the enemy, and a fire opened on the canoes would speedily sink them.

"Men, we are lost. Brown has failed to cross the river. If we could retreat we would, but that would mean death without glory. We must stand our ground and die with glory. Our country must never say we were cowards."

There was a suppressed cheer, and Allen knew that his few men were ready to make a determined stand.

Very soon they were to be put to the test.

The gates of the city were opened and a body of red-coated British regulars was seen to emerge; after them came two hundred Canadians, and an equal number of Indians.

The Americans saw they were outnumbered five to one.

"We will resist to the death!" Allen said to one of his officers, and the men heard the words and got ready to fight like brave heroes.

Although the British outnumbered the Americans five to one, they acted with the greatest caution, sheltering themselves behind woodpiles, houses and in ditches.

Allen's men returned the fire with vigor, and for two hours prevented the enemy from emerging into the open.

The British regulars began to be irritated at the stubborn resistance of the few Americans, and made a move which Allen knew was to be an attempt to flank him.

He called Capt. Lossier and bade him take fifty men and advance to the right and post himself in an advantageous ditch and to maintain his position there.

Lossier and his men advanced, but as soon as they came in sight of the redcoats they made a wild rush for the woods and scattered in all directions.

To make Allen's position worse, a small detachment on the left, under the command of Lieut. Young, a Canadian volunteer, also broke rank and fled, giving the enemy a chance to take up several strong positions.

Allen now found himself with only forty-five men, including the brave young Eben Pike.

They poured in their volleys as fast as they could load and fire.

In order to do more effective work five men were told off to load, and as the men who had run away had thrown down their muskets, there was a good chance to keep the guns cool.

But what could forty-five do against five hundred?

Allen saw that unless he retreated while his rear was open, he would be surrounded and all his men slaughtered, for he knew the command had gone out to butcher all found with arms in their hands.

With great reluctance he gave the order to retreat. The Indians were rapidly gaining in the direction of the rear, and only fleet feet would give the Americans a chance.

Although the Americans could run, they were no match for the Indians, and Allen found himself surrounded.

He had only twenty-eight men left, and yet he would not surrender.

With fixed bayonets the little band waited the onslaught of the British, who were only a few yards away on all sides.

An English captain, mad at the way in which his men had been kept at bay, snatched a musket from the hands of one of his men and fired at Allen.

Although only a few yards distant, the ball missed, and Allen, not to be thought wanting in reciprocal feelings, fired at the captain, but both were too much blown to take aim, so the shots were wasted.

"Coward!" shouted Allen—"cowards all! To think that it took five hundred men to capture twoscore patriots!"

The captain answered back and demanded surrender.

"As prisoners of war?" asked Allen.

"No. As rebels."

"Then, by the great Jehovah, I will die fighting! Men, let us resist to the death!"

To the surprise of the English, a volley was fired into their ranks, and the Americans prepared to load again.

Seven more of Allen's men had fallen wounded, while twelve of the English had been made to bite the dust.

"On what terms will you surrender?" asked the captain.

"That we shall all be recognized as prisoners of war and receive honorable treatment."

"On the word of a British officer, your terms shall be accepted."

The Americans threw down their arms.

As Allen presented his sword to the officer a naked savage, with hellish visage, made still more repulsive by the fact that half his head was shaved and the other half adorned with feathers, rushed at Allen and placed his musket at his head.

Allen caught the English captain and swung him between the Indian and himself, but the savage flew round with incredible swiftness and great fury, trying to kill the brave mountaineer without injuring the officer.

Allen succeeded in keeping the Englishman between him and the savage, but another Indian came rushing up and Allen gave all up as lost.

"Arrah, be jabers, if I can shtand that same!" shouted an Irishman in the service of England.

He rushed forward with fixed bayonet, risking punishment for breaking rank, and swearing by his forefathers that he would kill the "haythen," rescued Allen.

Thus, while Montgomery was waiting for him at St. John, Ethan Allen was a prisoner in the hands of the English and being marched into Montreal a captive.

In the barrack yard Gen. Prescott confronted him.

"Are you the Col. Allen who captured Ticonderoga?" he asked.

"I am."

A long string of expletives poured from the general's lips, and he swore that Allen should be shot.

He raised his cane to strike Allen across the face, but the Green Mountain Boy placed himself in fighting attitude.

"I am unarmed, you coward, but strike me and I will show you that my fists can smash your dastardly head."

An officer pulled the English general away, and Allen had no opportunity to avenge himself at that time.

"By Jove! I'll hang every one of you," shouted Gen. Prescott. "Colonel, see that thirteen of these d—d rebels are hanged within an hour; take the first thirteen—quick—there shall be no delay."

"If you dare to do it, I swear that you shall die within an hour after," shouted Allen, defiantly.

It was a strange threat for an unarmed prisoner to make.

CHAPTER XXVIII.
ON THE GASPEE.

Never before had English officer been spoken to in that manner by prisoner.

Prescott knew not what to make of it. Had he dared he would have shot Allen on the spot, but he well knew that to do so would be the cause of an investigation into his conduct, and Prescott was guilty of many things which, if sworn to before a court-martial, would have led to his dismissal from the army, if no other punishment was incurred.

So he allowed himself to be led away, but as he went he shook his fist at Allen and shouted:

"I will not hang them just now, but you, you infernal rebel, shall grace a halter at Tyburn."

Even the soldiers shuddered as they heard the threat, for Tyburn was the place, in England, where the most brutal murderers and criminals were hung in chains and allowed to stay there until their flesh rotted from their bones.

To be hung at Tyburn carried with it disgrace throughout all generations.

Gen. Prescott was in a fury; why, it was difficult to say, for Allen had never injured him personally.

"I'll hang that fellow," he reiterated to the colonel of his own regiment.

"My dear Prescott, you will do nothing of the kind; he is a prisoner of war."

"War be hanged! he is a rebel, not a soldier."

"And being a rebel, he must be tried by the home authorities."

"Col. Gilmartin, answer me; if he were to be on board a war ship and fall overboard and be drowned, could I be blamed?"

"Of course not."

"If by accident he should be given a dose of oxalic acid in mistake for Epsom salts, would that be charged against me?"

"What are you hinting at, general?"

"That fellow threatened me — —"

"He was exasperated."

"What right had he to be? A man who rebels should be ready for any treatment by his superiors. Hang me, if I dared, I would cut every rebel into pieces and send the parts to his friends with my compliments. They deserve such treatment. Hang me, what right have they to rebel?"

"They think they have a right."

"They think! Who are they? A lot of rapscalions who could not be content with their own country, but must come out here, and when we allow them to do so, they rebel. Englishmen worthy of the name never rebel."

"And yet, general, there were a good many worthy Englishmen who rebelled against James and supported William the Third."

"That was different, Gilmartin, different; they were patriots, and not rebels."

"As these men will be if they are successful."

"But they cannot be successful—they cannot be. This fellow, Allen, was a farmer. He calls himself colonel. Fancy, of the same rank as you, Gilmartin, while you were trained in your boyhood for the army, and when you were old enough got a commission——"

"Which I purchased, as I have had to every promotion."

Col. Gilmartin felt sore over his tardy promotions, and never waited a second opportunity to tell his grievances.

Prescott had been one of the fortunates ones; he had obtained his promotion easily, so he was satisfied with the condition of the army.

He was in no humor to listen to any complaints, and so he stopped his brother officer by saying:

"Order at once the placing of that fellow, Allen, in the heaviest irons—stay, I will give the order myself."

He sent for his orderly and gave instructions for Allen to be placed in heavy irons and taken at once on board the *Gaspee*, war ship, and all the other prisoners to be ironed and placed on board the other ships in the river.

The soldiers were pleased with the order, and proceeded to carry it out to the extreme limit.

Ordinary handcuffs were used for the wrists, two prisoners being manacled together, Allen being fortunate in having Eben for his fellow.

But on the legs the irons were simply horrible.

Anklets, very tight, were locked on each leg, and attached, in the middle of the connecting chain, to a bar of iron weighing forty pounds.

The soldiers laughed as they fastened this heavy weight on Allen's legs, telling him that it was the "king's plate."

The irons were so close that it was impossible for the prisoner to lie in any position save on his back.

Allen and Eben were taken to the lowest deck of the schooner *Gaspee*, and a more stifling, filthy, ill-ventilated place it would be impossible to find.

A mock salute was tendered to the hero of Ticonderoga as he entered the place, and out of consideration of his rank he was accorded a tool chest on which to sit, and which was also to serve as sleeping place.

"Can I help you any?" whispered the guard, about an hour after Allen had been placed on the chest.

"I wish you could get me some little blocks of wood to rest the iron on," answered Allen, gratefully.

The man secured the blocks and so saved the constant strain of forty pounds of iron pulling at the victim's legs.

While the men were kind and considerate, those in authority were just the reverse.

Every indignity possible was heaped on the unfortunate prisoners.

It was midnight, on the first day of Allen's imprisonment, and the Americans had managed to fall asleep.

Eben was lying at Allen's feet, enduring the most horrible tortures because of the irons, but never complaining for fear that he might be separated from his hero.

Suddenly their sleep was disturbed by a loud voice asking where the rebels had been placed.

It was the captain's voice, and he knew well, for he had ordered every detail.

"They are here, captain."

"Let them stand up."

Allen rose with difficulty, and staggered as he tried to stand at "attention."

"Drunk, eh? Here, sergeant, see to it that this rebel does not have a drop of anything to drink for twenty-four hours."

"Except water, captain?"

"I said not a drop of anything. He is drunk."

"Please, sir, he has had nothing to——"

"Silence! Do you want to be ordered to the hold?"

The sergeant was silent, though his whole nature rebelled against such treatment.

The captain looked at Allen for a minute, then he asked:

"You were at Ticonderoga?"

"And I treated the prisoners with justice," answered Allen.

The only reply was a vigorous kick from the officer's well-shod foot.

Allen bit his lips, but did not resent the affront.

He knew that it was done to provoke him so that his persecutors might have an excuse for inflicting some terrible punishment on him.

"See to it that these rebels do not sit down until I give permission."

It was the parting order of the captain, and the sergeant blushed with shame as he heard the command.

When the officer left the deck Allen sat down.

"You must not do that, sir," said the sergeant, kindly; "you heard my orders."

"I know, but I shall die unless — —"

"Lie down, sir; I shall not stop you doing that. The orders were that you must not sit."

Once more the two prisoners were lying down on their backs; the irons prevented their reposing on their sides.

By daylight the prisoners were nearly dead with thirst, but not a drop of water was allowed them.

The captain made his round of inspection at seven o'clock, and Allen asked if they were to be allowed to have anything to eat or drink.

"No. You will get a rope round your necks soon, and it won't matter whether you are hungry or not."

"But, sir, you have no right — —"

"Stay, there! You are a rebel and have forfeited all right to be considered in the matter."

Eben listened to the insulting words, and he was in such a position that he was able to drag his iron bar right across the captain's path.

As the officer stepped back he tripped over the iron and fell sprawling on the deck.

"Beg your pardon, captain, but I am not accustomed to move about with a bar of iron on my leg, so couldn't tell where it was going to land."

Eben spoke so seriously that even the captain thought it might have been an accident; so, after cursing the young Vermonter, he left the place.

Then Eben laughed heartily.

"Forfeited all right, have we? Well, I have found one way of humbling an Englishman."

"Eben, you ought not to have done it."

"Ought not? Why, I only regretted that we were not near enough to the side so that he would have fallen into the water."

"Hush!"

"You are not to have anything to drink, nor anything to eat, but hang me if I'm going to see you starve, so here, stow this into your mouth and suck like mad."

The kind-hearted sergeant pushed a piece of hard boiled beef into Allen's mouth.

Allen was too good a hunter not to know that the beef was prepared in such a way that, though tasteless, it nourished, and by sucking on it the saliva was promoted and thirst quenched.

After Eben had been served in the same way the sergeant laughed.

"I didn't give you aught to drink, nor aught to eat, but you'll get there all the same, and I ain't broken the rule."

"If ever I get the chance to remember your kindness, my memory will serve me."

"That's all right. I expect you'll get hanged, but blow me if I could see a dog starve, and you're a trump anyway, though you be a rebel."

CHAPTER XXIX.
ARRIVAL IN ENGLAND.

Three days after his capture, Ethan Allen heard an extraordinary noise on the upper deck, and he knew that the *Gaspee* was about to sail. But its destination he did not know.

After the first day the prisoners were allowed to have one meal a day, for, as Prescott told Allen, he did not want to cheat the gallows.

The *Gaspee* was bound for Quebec, and the prisoners were overjoyed at the prospect of a change.

"It cannot be for the worse," said one of the Americans to Allen; "therefore we shall be the gainers."

"I wish they would hang us right away," answered the hero of Ticonderoga, "for I am tired of this life."

"We shall all be free — —"

"Yes, when in our graves."

"Do not get downhearted, colonel; we have pulled through many a hard row before now."

There was a consolation in having company, and the prisoners from the other ships had been crowded on the *Gaspee.*

"March out the rebels."

All heard the order given, and each looked at his fellow with anxious glance.

It might be a farewell to them. Who could tell?

The leg irons were unlocked and the prisoners marched up the companionway to the upper deck.

As they reached the deck the fresh air was almost overwhelming, for they had not breathed any for several days.

They were marshaled in line and awaited their doom.

Soon a bedecked officer appeared on deck accompanied by one of the most villainous-looking seamen that ever stepped upon a deck.

"Are these all?" asked the English officer.

"Yes, general."

"Which is Ethan Allen?"

Allen was pointed out, and the gold-laced, red-coated officer raised his pince-nez and looked at Allen as he would at any curiosity.

"Which is Eben Pike?"

The young scout was pointed out by the officer in charge, and he had to undergo a similar inspection.

"And these are rebels? Well, well! England has nothing to fear if this is a sample of those fighting against her. So you are Ethan Allen? You are the man who broke into Ticonderoga? Well, well, well! You achieved fame, but whether it will avail you much when you stand on the gallows is for you to say."

The English officer had jerked out these sentences more to himself than to the prisoners.

He turned to the villainous old salt by his side.

"What do you think of your cargo?"

"I'd rather have pigs."

"You show sense, but as you cannot have pigs you must take these. You are under bonds to land them in England—how I don't care— only they must have strength enough to stand upright on the gallows, for Jack Ketch must not have too great a task."

The seaman chuckled.

"I've carried lots of cattle afore, and I never lose any, save a few I toss overboard to save trouble. I'll land these or give an account of 'em."

Every word was uttered with a view of enraging the prisoners.

Allen learned afterward that the provocation was intended and deliberate, its object being to get him to commit some overt act so that he could be hanged or shot for insubordination.

The seaman was the captain of a sailing merchantman bound for England, who had been engaged to transport the Americans to that country.

After a list had been made of the prisoners they were marched off the *Gaspee* onto a barge, which was towed out to a merchantman lying in the bay. Four rowboats were engaged to tow the barge, and just as they started the hawser broke and the barge was adrift.

After several minor accidents the prisoners were landed on the deck of the merchantman, and soon found they had exchanged bad for worse.

A portion of the vessel had been boarded off by white oak planks, making a space about twenty-two feet long by twenty feet wide.

Into this space thirty-four American prisoners were pushed, handcuffed in pairs.

Allen refused to enter.

The captain asked who he was that he should dare to disobey orders.

"I surrendered to the British under a pledge that I should be treated as a prisoner of war, and I demand that we shall all be treated as human beings, not as cattle."

The captain laughed brutishly.

"Ha! ha! ha! That is good! Do you think I would treat cattle that way? They would all be dead before they reached England. No, no, my dear rebel! you are treated as rebels, not cattle."

Two seamen took hold of Allen and threw him into the little inclosure, closing the door as soon as he was within.

An hour later Allen was called out.

A lieutenant had asked to see him.

"So you are Ethan Allen?" the English lieutenant asked.

"That is my name."

"Then, apart from the pleasure I have in seeing you here, I have but one greater joy, and that is that I am able to treat you like this."

The officer spat in Allen's face.

The Green Mountain hero's hands were manacled, but he raised them and brought them down with such force on the man's face that he fell headlong on the deck.

Instantly Allen was surrounded with bayonets.

He was considered dangerous, and had to be forced back into the prison inclosure.

The vessel set sail, and every day the captain taunted the prisoners with their captivity, and took every means to make them suffer.

Some days, when the weather was more than ordinarily oppressive, he would order that no water should be given, and as the food consisted of salt pork and bread, or ship's biscuit, it can be well imagined how much they all suffered.

After the vessel had been out twenty days one of the prisoners crawled up to Allen and whispered into his ear:

"Can we live much longer like this?"

"I am afraid not."

"Then let us put an end to it."

"How?"

"Will you agree to join us?"

"I cannot answer that until I know what is proposed."

"If you do not want to join, you will not betray us?"

"What do you think of me? Have I ever been a sneak?"

"No, colonel, but the scheme is a desperate one."

"What is it?"

"To seize the ship and then take her into port as a captured vessel."

"How can it be done?"

"Jack—you know Jack, the one who brings us tobacco?"

"Yes; he is a kind-hearted Englishman."

"He isn't English, he is Irish. Now, he will file off these handcuffs and give me the file. By working at every opportunity we can all be free in a few days; then all we have to do is to force our way out and seize the skipper. We will throw him overboard, and kill all who oppose us; then the ship will be ours and we can sell it and divide the prize money."

"My good fellow, we cannot do it."

"Why?"

"If we seized the ship we should have to sink it, for no one would purchase it. But I will not countenance murder."

"It is not murder, it is war."

"War is brutal, I know, but when it comes to seizing a captain on board his own vessel and killing him, that is not war, but murder, or piracy."

"Well, you will not betray us?"

"No. Only give me a chance to fight openly and I will do so, but I will not kill a man in cold blood."

"But, colonel, you will not interfere with us?"

"No. Only do not tell me anything you are doing."

Allen did not understand that in war all things were justifiable.

He was a gentleman all the way through, and would not fight unless he could do so honorably.

Whether Jack failed to find the file, or that the prisoners decided not to mutiny, Allen never knew, but no attempt was ever made to secure freedom, and after forty days' torture land was sighted.

The prisoners were ordered on deck.

It was a glorious change for them, for they had not breathed a breath of pure air for forty days.

As they stood on the deck the captain pointed out the distant land.

"Do you know what land that is?" he asked.

There was no response; the American prisoners were too much engaged in inhaling all the fresh air they could to care about talking.

"That is Land's End, in England. You will soon be there, and then you will all be hanged. A short life and a wretched one will be yours from now on. That is all. Take the prisoners back to their palatial quarters."

The captain may have thought he was inflicting torture on the prisoners, but he was mistaken. They were not afraid of the fate which awaited them.

If they were to die, they would prefer to die on land to being tortured to death in the hold of a small ship.

As one of the prisoners quoted the words of an older rebel in England:

"The noblest place for man to die
Is where he dies for man."

So all felt that if they were to be hanged in England they would be tried, and on their trial they would be able to make their defense and let the world know under what grievances the American colonies were suffering.

In two days the vessel landed in Falmouth Harbor.

The news that the vessel had on board a number of American prisoners caused thousands of people to flock to the wharf.

The greatest curiosity was manifested.

Had a cargo of wild beasts entered port the curiosity could not have been greater.

In fact, Allen soon learned that the Americans were looked upon as wild beasts or savages, and certainly not as civilized beings.

The windows were filled with members of the fair sex, the sidewalks of the old English town were closely packed by men and children.

Hour after hour they waited to see the show.

A lot of detail, commonly called "red tape," had to be attended to before the prisoners were allowed to land.

A military band escorted a regiment of redcoats down to the dock, and the necessary papers for the transfer of the prisoners were exchanged.

Then across the gangplank walked Ethan Allen and Eben Pike, handcuffed together.

The people on the dock pushed and stared at the Green Mountain men.

"Why, they aren't green!" exclaimed one of the bystanders with disgust.

"No, they aren't Americans; they're Irish," said another.

"Of course they're Irish; Americans are black."

"No, red."

"Not by a long shot; they're all as yellow as guineas."

Absurd as it may appear at this day to have to record such ideas, it is an absolute fact that when it was rumored that the Green Mountain heroes were on their way to England the prevalent idea was that they derived their name from the color of their skin.

When the other prisoners disembarked the march was commenced to the barracks.

The people flocked round the prisoners so that progress was impeded.

The soldiers had to charge the crowd with bayonets many times.

"What did they mean by saying they thought we were Irish?" asked Eben. "I heard an Englishman say in New York that if it had not been for the Irish the Americans would not have rebelled. Of course it was nonsense, but the people do not know us yet, while they do know the Irish."

At the barracks the prisoners were received with as much curiosity as we can imagine was shown by Ferdinand and Isabella when Columbus presented the American Indians in 1492.

Every man was made to answer a lot of questions, and many times over.

Allen was questioned about the strength of the American army, and replied:

"I know not its numbers, but it is well equipped and can beat all the armies you can send over there."

"They are rebels, and only the lowest people sympathize with them."

"Do you call George Washington a common man?" asked Allen.

"He is a rebel, and ought to know better."

"And Richard Montgomery, who fought with you at Havana and Martinique?"

"Is he with the rebels?"

"I had the honor of serving under him."

"He will be hanged, for he was a soldier of his majesty."

"You will have to capture him first."

They could not make anything of Allen, so they desisted questioning and sent all the prisoners to the guardroom.

It was a difficult question for the government of England to decide.

The men were locked up in the barracks at Falmouth, but England did not know what to do with them.

If the prisoners were hanged as rebels, England would be blamed by other civilized nations, and yet it would not do to pardon them.

There was a very powerful opposition among the English people to harsh measures, and, in fact, many English wished America success in its struggle with the tory ministry.

And so Allen and his friends remained in jail, simply because the ministry did not know what to do with them.

CHAPTER XXX.
IRISH HOSPITALITY.

Some months later the ministry decided to deport the American prisoners, and the captain of the *Solebay*, man-of-war, was ordered to take the prisoners back to America under sealed orders.

It was a pleasant change to leave the barrack prison, even for captivity on board a man-of-war.

Gradually the strictness had relaxed and the prisoners were treated better, and Allen fully believed that the meaning of the return to America was that they were to be liberated in exchange.

The master of arms on the *Solebay* was an Irishman named Michael Gilligan, and the vessel had only been out two nights when Gilligan sought Allen and offered him his friendship.

"And it's meself as would be a rebel if I were free, but, bad cess to it, I was pressed, and so I made the best of a bad job, and will fight for the flag because it is my duty."

"I admire a brave Englishman——" Allen commenced, but was cut short with the remark:

"I'm not an Englishman, but I'm Irish, and my people are all rebels. Will ye let me be your friend?"

"I shall be only too pleased."

"Then you'll berth with me. Sure it's not such a place as I'd like to be offering you, but it's better than this."

Gilligan held a similar rank to that of a sergeant of a regiment, and was a man of considerable importance on board.

He had a berth between decks, inclosed in canvas, and, as it was large, Allen had plenty of room.

When Cork, or rather the Cove of Cork, now called Queenstown, was reached and the *Solebay* cast anchor, the rumor spread through the cove that a number of American rebels were on board.

Allen was standing on deck looking over the finest harbor in Europe, when his attention was called to a small boat hailing the war ship.

Some men climbed up on deck and asked for Col. Allen, of America.

Allen was so close that he could not help hearing, and he answered that he was Ethan Allen.

John Hays, a merchant of Cork, clasped Allen's hand and tried to speak, but, instead of words, tears flowed down his cheeks and his voice was choked.

When he did master his emotion he exclaimed, with patriarchal fervor:

"Heaven bless you and all brave men like you who are fighting for liberty."

He introduced his friend, merchant Clark, also of Cork, and said their mission was to offer the patriots such things as they stood in need of.

Clothes, or money, or food would be willingly given if Allen would only say what was most needed.

The offer was gratifying, and Allen expressed a wish for clothes for the prisoners. He explained that, though prisoners for several months, they had not received a change of clothes, and that some were absolutely in rags.

The next day a boat well laden pulled to the *Solebay*, and suits of clothes were found for each of the thirty-four prisoners.

A complete suit of underwear, an outer suit of warm material, an overcoat and two extra shirts, were bestowed on each of the prisoners, while Allen received superfine broadcloth sufficient for two jackets, and two pairs of breaches, in addition to a suit already made. He also received eight fine Holland shirts and socks ready made, a number of pairs of silk hose, two pairs of shoes, two beaver hats, one of which, richly laced with gold, came from James Bonwell, a wealthy merchant of Cork.

On the following day the boat returned to the ship laden with wines, spirits, sugar, tea and chocolate, a large round of picked beef, a number of fat turkeys and many other articles for Allen's personal use, while each of the men received two pounds of tea and six pounds of sugar, with plenty of meat, chickens and turkeys for the mess table of the prisoners.

Two days after the receipt of the stores the captain prohibited anything more being delivered to the prisoners, and took away everything which the men of Cork had given except the clothing.

He shouted himself hoarse about the way the rebels were being feasted.

"I heard him say," says Ethan Allen, in his autobiography, "that by all that was holy the American rebels should not be feasted by the rebels of Ireland."

An application was made by the Mayor of Cork for permission to be granted to Ethan Allen to attend a banquet to be given in his honor by the city, the mayor and ten leading citizens being willing to give bond for his return to the ship the next morning.

The application was refused, and the captain gave order to weigh anchor and put out to sea.

"Sure and the skipper is as hot as a roast pertater," said Gilligan; "he thinks for sure that the rebels of Cork will take you all off the ship by force, so he is going to put out to sea."

The *Solebay* left Cork harbor that day and did not return.

After a long sail the shore of North Carolina was reached, and the hearts of the Americans beat high with hope.

The captain was almost amiable, but it was with a fiendish glee caused by the belief that the American prisoners were to be hanged on American soil.

"I want to see," he said, to Allen, "American trees bearing the best fruit, and plenty of it."

"I am sure I re-echo your wish," answered Allen, whereupon the captain laughed and declared that the fruit he meant was dead Americans hanging from the boughs.

For several weeks the *Solebay* stayed at Cape Fear, and the prisoners were treated with great harshness.

One morning their hopes were again raised by an order for all to appear on deck.

"Stand in line!" ordered the officer.

The men did so and the roll was called.

"Colonel Allen, step forward!"

It was the first time he had been addressed by his title, and all thought it meant an exchange at least.

"Now select fifteen of the most deserving men among your company, and order them to stand out."

Allen selected the desired number.

"Thank you, Col. Allen. The fifteen will remain, the others can go below. The fifteen will be hanged to-morrow morning at sunrise. I thank you in the name of his majesty for having selected the most worthy."

CHAPTER XXXI.
A DARING SWIM.

"Coward!"

It was only one word, but that one word contained a wealth of contempt and scorn which made the officer tremble.

"Place those men in chains!"

The sergeant of marines saluted and gave the order to the remaining prisoners to return to their prison place.

Allen countermanded the order.

"Listen to me. I am a freeborn man, and, though a prisoner, I am a prisoner of war. I was promised fair treatment for myself and men if we would surrender at Quebec. Is this what you call fair treatment?"

"I am very sorry for you, Col. Allen; but, since I am a soldier, I am compelled to obey orders."

"And who gave you such an order?"

"That I may not answer—as you ought to know, being a soldier yourself."

"Are these men to be hanged?"

"So I was ordered to say. I have only acted according to instructions."

It was the man that spoke, not the officer. His softened voice showed that he had carried out a very distasteful order, and that his manhood revolted at it.

"Can I not make an appeal personally to the general commanding?"

"That would be impossible."

"Are these men to be hanged without trial?"

"Col. Allen, you are a brave man, and can face the worst. I am told, though I ought not to tell you, that the American rebels have gained several advantages lately, and the British authorities are determined to stamp out the rebellion; so——" He paused. The man was ashamed to utter what he had heard. Gathering courage from Allen's silence he continued: "We are told that no prisoners are to be treated as prisoners of war, but as outlaws and rebels, to shoot whom will be considered a meritorious act."

"And the object?"

"Can you not see? It is to strike terror into the rebels."

"So be it! But, mark me, I speak as a rebel, but also as a man, and I tell you that for every American hanged without due process of law, ten Englishmen shall die. Do not mistake me! I shall be a free man again, and shall make England suffer. The leaders of the Americans, called by you rebels, will know of this murder and will avenge it."

The British officer made no reply, but waved his hand to the sergeant, who removed the ill-fated fifteen.

By some chance Allen had omitted Eben's name from the fifteen, and while he regretted it at first, he was more than pleased now that the oversight had occurred.

When the prisoners were removed to their part of the lower deck, Eben managed to get close to Allen.

"You don't think they will hang those?" he asked.

"I do not know, my boy. I think they are vile enough for anything."

"I heard that officer, who came aboard with dispatches, say that there was a lot of the patriots close here."

"Of our people?"

"Yes."

"That accounts for it, then. They will hang the prisoners as an act of defiance."

"Colonel, I have an idea."

"What is it, Eben?"

"Come closer to me, for I must whisper very softly."

Eben managed so that his mouth was very close to Allen's ear, and then he told of his plan.

"I can slip over into the water when it is quite dark and swim to land; then I can make my way to the patriots and tell them the straits we are in."

"You could not reach the land."

"Not reach it? Why, colonel, have you forgotten how I swam across dear old Champlain and then back again?"

"I am not likely to forget that."

"Then I am sure I can do this little bit."

"But they will fire on you?"

"If they see me; and that is just what I am going to prevent."

"How?"

"Never mind that, colonel. Only give your consent and I will succeed, and I think I can save the lives of our friends."

"Eben, you are very brave. Can you bear to think of your fate?"

"I have thought of it. If we stay here we shall be hanged; if I fail to reach land I shall drown, and I think I would rather drown than be hanged. What say you, colonel?"

"My dear fellow, you must act as you think best."

"All right, colonel. Good-by; I may never see you again."

"Good-by, Eben. Take care of yourself, and may Heaven bless you."

Several times Allen tried to communicate with Eben, and to try to dissuade him from his hazardous undertaking, but the youth felt instinctively that he would do so, and remained out of reach of his beloved colonel's voice.

When night came Eben managed to get to the side of the ship unobserved, and in a few moments he had dropped noiselessly into the water.

But, as ill luck would have it, he got entangled in some chains as he struck out from the ship, and the noise attracted the attention of the guard.

"Man overboard!" he cried.

Allen heard the cry and his heart stood still, for he was sure Eben would be captured, and then nothing could save his life.

The officer in charge of the prisoners heard the cry also, and at once ordered every man to answer to his name.

It was the work of but a few minutes, and it was ascertained that Eben had really escaped.

"Do you see him?" asked the captain.

"Yes."

"Fire on him!"

Several muskets were fired, and had not the Vermonter been an excellent swimmer he would have been killed. But Eben dived and swam under the water a great distance, and the bullets were deflected by the water.

A boat was lowered and the stoutest sailors, with four marines, manned it.

"Ten pounds to the man who kills him," said the captain, "and twenty for the man who brings him in alive."

There was a stimulus in the offer of reward, although the Englishmen, every one of them, would have gloried in the chase and in hunting the boy to his death without even the chance of a reward.

Eben saw the boat coming after him, and he knew that he was in a race for life.

He was not daunted.

He watched the boat skim through the moonlit water, and he floated for some little distance to ascertain whether he was seen.

Assured of that, he laughed quietly to himself over the chase he would give them.

He dashed the water about as though he was about to sink, and instantly a musket ball struck the water within a few feet of him.

Then he dived and swam in another direction, knowing that the boat would continue on its straight track.

When he reappeared above the water he saw that he had gained very materially on his pursuers, and as he did not care what part of the coast he reached, he again dived and swam farther down the shore.

When he came to the surface and floated, he looked round and saw that the boat's crew had given him up for lost.

The boat was circling round and round, and every eye was strained to find his dead body.

Eben leisurely swam to the shore, and was glad when he reached land, for he was nigh exhausted.

He had to be very cautious, for many tories resided on the shore, and he knew that he would be treated as a suspicious character.

He found a wood which afforded him shelter.

Undressing, he hung his clothes out to dry, while he climbed into a tree, with the double object of not being found in a state of undress and be the better able to see if anyone approached.

There was a warm breeze blowing, and his clothes soon dried, and once again he felt like a human being.

A new trouble arose. He found his limbs so weak that he could not stand.

His flesh was hot and dry, his mouth parched, and his eyes were like burning coals.

He had fever.

The fact was appalling enough at ordinary times, but how much more so under the circumstances?

He dare not seek a house, even if he could crawl as far, for he knew that fever meant delirium, and in his delirium he might betray himself and so injure the cause he loved so well.

He had not lived in the mountains without knowing the value of herbs, so he looked around to find those natural medicines which at home had been used by the Indians and most of the white folks of the Green Mountains.

He wanted agrimony, but did not see any; but he did find yarrow in abundance.

Now, the leaves and flowers of the common yarrow, or the *achillea milefolium* of botanists, are an excellent thing in fevers, producing perspiration and cleansing the blood at the same time; but Eben knew that it should be macerated in boiling water.

Boiling water was out of the question, and, in fact, there seemed to be no water save sea water near, so he gathered a quantity of the leaves and chewed them. The taste was bitter and aromatic, but refreshing to the fever-stricken boy.

After a time he felt a nausea, and stopped eating.

He turned over on his back and fell asleep.

When he awoke the sun was high in the heavens and he fancied he had slept four or five hours; in reality he had slept nearly thirty hours.

His body was covered with a cold perspiration and his mouth seemed less parched.

As he raised himself to look around he saw that he was not alone.

A man, evidently poor, if judged by his dress, stood some distance away, watching him closely.

"So you did wake, eh? I reckon'd that you were going to sleep till Gabriel blew his trump."

"Have I slept long?" asked Eben.

"Well, now, I can't say 'zactly, for I reckon you had been asleep a long time when I found you, and I've been here nigh on to ten hours."

"You have been watching me that long? Why?"

"Mebbe I took a fancy to you, and mebbe I know you."

"You know me?"

"Well, now, I reckon if I were to call you Ebenezer Pike——"

"If you did?"

"Yes, I was saying I reckon that you would have to say that was your name."

"What gave you that idea? And who is Ebenezer Pike?"

"I am no tory. Yesterday I heard that a prisoner had escaped from the war ship out there, and that the one who had got away was at the bottom of the sea. I was curious, and I asked all about it. Then I was asked if a body wouldn't float into land; and I said mebbe; and then the bluejacket told me he would give me ten shillings if I found the body and gave it up to him. So I searched and found—you."

"And discovered that I was not worth ten shillings?"

"Never mind what I found; I tell you I ain't no tory, and ten pounds, nor ten hundred pounds, would make me give up a live American hero. His dead body wouldn't be of no account to him, so I might give up that."

"And you think I am this escaped prisoner! Well, what do you want to do with me? for I am too weak to oppose your silly whim."

"I am going to take you to my house, and when you get strong you shall go just where you please."

"You mean this?"

"I do; and I tell you that if we could liberate Col. Ethan Allen we would, for he is wanted just now; Carolina means to be free and independent, so it does."

Eben did not attempt any resistance; in fact, he was too weak to oppose his discoverer, so he allowed himself to be lifted on the man's shoulder and be carried to a cabin on the other side of the wood.

Here he was tended as well as if he had been among relatives or his friends of the Green Mountains.

After a few days he was strong enough to go out, and he walked down to the beach and saw the vessel from which he had escaped lying at anchor.

But he saw something more—something which made his blood run cold.

As he was returning he saw five trees growing on the banks of the river near the cape, and from each tree there dangled a human body.

On closer inspection he found—what he had dreaded to find—that the bodies were those of some of his fellow prisoners.

"Come away, my boy," said his new friend. "Those men gave their lives for a sacred cause, and I wish every Carolinian could see and know them. It is a good thing for us that the cowardly tories hanged them, for every one hanged means a surer vengeance."

"It is horrible! Will they dare to serve Col. Allen so?"

"I don't think so, but they may. What are your plans?"

"I want to find the army of America and get the men to liberate Col. Allen."

"Praiseworthy, but we shall have a weary tramp before we reach the patriots. Things have changed and many difficulties will confront us."

"You say 'us,' as though you were going?"

"Where you go, so shall I."

Once more the two walked down to the beach, and Eben gave a cry of pain as he saw the war ship slowly sailing away.

CHAPTER XXXII.
HOW ENGLAND TREATED PRISONERS OF WAR.

After Eben had escaped the captain of the war ship was furious.

He found out that five of the prisoners shared the same room with the escaped one, and he closely questioned them about the escape. They refused to speak a word; perhaps they knew nothing, but their mouths were closely sealed.

Orders were given to take the five prisoners to the shore and hang them in such a conspicuous place that the rebels might see them and take warning.

This cruel and uncivilized act was carried out by men who loathed the work, but who had to obey the orders of their superior.

Fearing that unpleasantness might ensue from the order, which, when too late, the captain regretted, orders were given to sail north, and Ethan Allen was taken to New York, where he was landed and thrown into a prison cell.

While it was a change to be on land, the treatment was more severe.

Every indignity was heaped upon the unfortunate prisoners by the tories who ruled the city.

There was but one gleam of sunshine in the hero's life.

He often heard news of the outside world.

A Congress had been called, and its deliberations were of vital importance.

The tories talked about it in Allen's presence.

They denounced men whose names Allen had not heard before, but who were becoming prominent. But they also talked of Sam Adams and John Hancock, of Patrick Henry and George Washington, and then they told each other that it was seriously proposed to create a new nation out of the colonies and declare the independence of the colonies.

All this was glorious news to the prisoner, and he listened in silence, afraid that his joy, if known, would prevent further conversation in his presence.

One hot, stifling day in July there was considerable commotion in the prison, and Allen knew that something more than the ordinary had caused the excitement.

How anxiously he waited to hear the news!

How tedious the hours passed before the change of guards gave the desired few minutes for conversation.

At last the hour came!

"The Declaration of Independence has been signed!"

"You do not mean it? The rebels would never dare!"

"But they have dared. They say that a new nation has been born. Ha, ha, ha! He, he, he! Ha, ha, ha!"

"Will all the prisoners have to be shot now?"

"No, they will be hanged, same as before. England has not recognized the new nation; but England has hired a lot of Hessians—
—"

"What are they?"

"Don't you know? They come from some place in Europe; their king sells or leases them out to fight."

"And they must fight whether they like it or not?"

"Oh, they like fighting; they are trained to fight. It is the only thing they can do, and they do it well. You see, they do it all the better because they can't talk English, so they kill all who do——"

"Then they may kill us."

"No, I do not mean that, but they kill all they are told to kill."

A warden entered the long corridor and called out the name of Ethan Allen.

Allen stepped from his cell and submitted to his arms and legs being heavily ironed.

He was then marched through the city to the Battery, where he was placed on board a war ship, with other prisoners, and taken to Halifax.

For nearly two years he suffered the most horrible tortures in prisons and prison ships. He seemed to have been forgotten.

For weeks at a time he was absolutely silent, no one being allowed to speak to him, and silence was strictly enforced among the prisoners.

Once Allen got a little paper and a pencil, and a friendly jailer promised to have the letter sent to its destination.

Allen addressed it to his brother at Bennington, in the Green Mountains, and it duly reached its destination, but the brother was away with the patriot army, the letter was kept, however, and read over and over again by the old friends of the hero of Ticonderoga.

In that letter he says:

"I have seen American patriot prisoners begging for food and being laughed at for their request. They have bitten pieces of wood to get little chips to eat and so satisfy their hunger. I was imprisoned for a time in a church, watched over by Hessians who would not let us leave to satisfy the wants of nature, and mid excrements the poor wretches, who only loved their country, died in horrible tortures."

It was a wonder that the letter ever reached Bennington, but the jailer who passed it out was a warm-hearted man, a son of the soil from Ireland.

It was in the early spring of 1778 that Allen heard his name called as he sat in the hold of a war ship lying off New York.

He dragged his legs wearily up the steps to the deck.

He had aged much during those two years, and his friends would scarcely have known him.

As he reached the deck he heard a voice, which seemed very familiar, say:

"Colonel, don't you know me?"

A tall, bearded young man stood before him with extended hand.

"Eben!"

"Ah! then I have not changed so much."

It was Eben Pike, dressed in the uniform of a lieutenant of the American army.

"What brings you here? You are not a prisoner?"

"No; at this moment I am a guest of His Majesty the King of England, and am acting on behalf of the United States of America, and more especially the commander-in-chief, Gen. Washington, and— —"

"I am so glad to see you, Eben, that I do not know what you have been saying. I feared you were dead."

"No, colonel, I had a work to do, and I have done it. You see, we, that is, the American army, took a certain English colonel prisoner, and England wanted him very badly, so Gen. Washington said: 'You shall have him in exchange for Col. Ethan Allen,' and at last the order for the exchange was made and you are free."

What did it mean?

Allen heard the word "free," but it seemed like an echo of fairyland, having nothing in common with this matter-of-fact, cruel world.

"Yes, Col. Allen, you are free."

This time the word was spoken by an English officer.

Allen staggered like a drunken man, and would have fallen had not Eben caught him.

"Come, colonel, we must not trespass on the hospitality of the King of England any longer; I have promised to escort you with all due diligence to the headquarters of the commander-in-chief."

Allen stood still, looking, with glassy eyes, at the speaker.

In a few moments he asked;

"Am I dreaming?"

"It looked very like it, colonel, for you acted as though you were asleep; but come now, we must be going."

"Do you mean it? Are you really Eben Pike?"

"Ask the captain here. He will vouch for that. The document reads: 'The bearer, Lieut. Pike, of the Army of the United States of America,' does it not?"

"Yes, Col. Allen, the whole thing means that you are exchanged. We have got our man, and we pay for his liberty by giving you yours. Good-day, and may I never see you again—at least under recent conditions."

Allen entered a small boat with Eben, and two stout seamen pulled the boat to the dock, where a carriage was in waiting.

Eben almost pushed the astonished and half-dazed Green Mountain hero into the carriage, and soon the waterside was left far behind and the carriage rolled along the roads to the place where Gen. Washington had made his headquarters.

By that time Allen had begun to realize that he was really free.

Washington met him at the door and grasped his hand warmly.

"For over a year we have been trying to secure your release, but could not get the English to consent. You have to thank Lieut. Eben Pike for your release. He is a real hero."

"General, I only did my duty."

"I wish every soldier did his duty as well. I must tell Col. Allen; I am sure he will be prouder than ever."

"No, general, it was a mere nothing."

"I am the best judge of that. You must understand, colonel, that Pike enlisted in the cavalry and did excellent service as a private soldier; he was speedily promoted, for he deserved it. But it was at the battle of White Plains that he distinguished himself. Almost single-handed he fought a company of cavalry when most of our men had retreated. He was surrounded and refused to surrender. 'I have been a prisoner of England once,' he said, and that was enough for him. He cut his way through the enemy, and even that enemy has borne testimony to his great bravery. I am proud of him."

"I am sure that a braver man than my young friend, Pike, never drew sword," added Allen, proudly.

"After he had gallantly cut his way through the enemy, he says he thought he could have done better, so he turned his horse and rode after the British. They evidently thought that he was the advance guard of a regiment, for they stuck their rowels into the horses and rode for life. Pike followed up closely and overtook Col. Jameson; he demanded his surrender, and Jameson had to submit, for Pike had the advantage."

"Yes, he could not help himself and live," Eben said, with a smile.

"Pike took his captive into camp, and the affair was reported to me. Sergt. Pike became lieutenant, but he was not satisfied. He knew that Jameson was a most important personage, almost as valuable as Cornwallis himself, so what does the young lieutenant do but ask me to refuse to exchange Jameson unless you were the captive given up by the British. The difficulty had been that you had no commission; I did not know it until I heard it from Montgomery and Schuyler, and so the British looked upon you as an outsider; but they wanted Jameson, and they got him, and you owe your freedom to Pike's pertinacity."

We can easily imagine Allen's feelings as he listened to the account given by Washington.

The pride he had felt in Eben's career was intensified, and he felt that the young Green Mountain scout would become one of the great heroes of the Revolution.

Allen was so broken down by his long and cruel imprisonment that he took a vacation and retired to Bennington to recuperate.

CHAPTER XXXIII.
BEVERLY ROBINSON'S OFFER.

As though the colonies had not enough work on hand in fighting the great power of Britain, they must needs quarrel among themselves, or at least New York picked a quarrel with New Hampshire over the title to Vermont.

Vermont was more than ever determined to remain independent of either New Hampshire or New York, and Ethan Allen admired the sturdy spirit of his mountaineers.

He was urged to take command of the Green Mountain forces, and he consented, writing Gen. Washington and telling him how he regretted the necessity of staying at home instead of entering the army of emancipation.

Washington replied in a friendly letter, reminding him that he deserved a rest after his trials, and also telling him that a man's first duty was to his own people and country.

Acting on this letter, Allen applied to the Congress for the admission of Vermont into the Confederation of States; but the rivals of New York and New Hampshire were too powerful in the councils of the new nation for Allen, and Vermont remained outside, a debatable territory.

Ethan Allen was sitting by the great, open fireplace in his house one evening in the early fall, when a visitor was announced.

"You have forgotten me, Col. Allen?"

"I do not remember having had the pleasure of your acquaintance."

"I am Beverly Robinson."

"Indeed! Ah, now I remember. May I ask what brought you here?"

The tory did not like the brusque question, but he was a diplomat and fenced ably.

"I have heard of your prowess on the field and of your sufferings in captivity, and I have felt that, though we differ in politics, we are children of the same mountains and ought to be friends."

"If you are loyal to Vermont, differences of opinion will not affect me."

"Spoken like the brave man I knew you to be."

"Did you come here to tell me this?"

"Partly, and more especially to discuss the future of Vermont."

"Ah!"

"Yes; we are in a strange predicament. We have cut loose from the mother country, and the new country will not have us."

"That is one way of looking at the matter."

"Is it not the true one?"

"It may be."

"Well, why not pledge ourselves to remain neutral?"

"To remain neutral?"

"Yes. If we were to call a convention and pass a resolution to the effect that in the war between England and the colonies—I beg pardon, States—Vermont would remain absolutely neutral, we should be in a good position."

"In what way?"

"England would protect us against New York, and we could protect ourselves against New Hampshire."

"And you would ask me to make terms with England?"

"Why not? You do not believe that Washington will succeed. He cannot. England will triumph. The best men feel that it will be so. Benedict Arnold told me it was only a question of time and terms."

"Indeed!"

"Yes; he knows that all Washington is fighting for now is to get the best terms he can from Great Britain."

"Arnold told you this?"

"Well, no, not exactly in those words. But let me carry to headquarters your pledge of neutrality."

"Mr. Robinson, you may be honest in this, but I am afraid you are being made a tool of some designing person. Carry this back with you"—Allen stood up and folded his arms defiantly, as he said: "Tell England that Ethan Allen will never be neutral, never make terms with England, but will fight her power as long as he lives! Good-day, and never enter my house again as the agent of England."

Beverly Robinson retired second in the contest. Allen had won.

Though the tory had failed, he felt a respect for Allen, who had been so bold and courageous, and, though Allen never knew it, he was the means of saving Vermont from any attacks of the British.

Allen served his State and defended it against enemies without and within. He lived to see it recognized as a State, free and independent.

He also witnessed, with shame, the treachery of Benedict Arnold, and was glad that he had never recognized the traitor as a man of honor.

In the annals of the Revolution the name of Ethan Allen will ever shine conspicuously, and, though he fought but few battles, and remained in the army but a few months, England hated the mention of his name, and looked upon him as one of the men who fired the hearts of the Americans and encouraged them in the demand for freedom.

In the hearts of his countrymen he will ever be held in the highest estimation, and all ages will greet the Green Mountain Boy as the "Hero of Ticonderoga."

THE END.

Lightning Source UK Ltd.
Milton Keynes UK
UKHW010635140621
385483UK00001B/36